D1147970

## GHOSTLY COMPANIONS

A figurehead that is more than it seems, a patchwork made like none other, a mirror image that never leaves you alone, a garden that no child should enter at night, a masquerade that gives you the chance to be someone else . . .

Vivien Alcock blends the ordinary and the extraordinary to make these stories all the more disquieting.

## ABOUT THE AUTHOR

Vivien Alcock was born in Worthing, Sussex, and moved to Wiltshire when she was ten. She studied at Oxford School of Art and worked in London as a commercial artist for several years. She also did odd jobs as an ambulance driver, secretary in a beauty salon and shop assistant in an antique shop.

Now she lives in Highgate in London with her husband, Leon Garfield, the well-known children's author, her daughter Jane and her dog and cat. She spends her time painting and writing.

*Other titles by Vivien Alcock in the New Windmill Series:*

A Kind of Thief
The Trial of Anna Cotman
The Monster Garden
The Cuckoo Sister

# VIVIEN ALCOCK

# – GHOSTLY –
# COMPANIONS

## 10 STORIES OF THE SUPERNATURAL

Heinemann
*New Windmills*

Heinemann Educational Publishers
Halley Court, Jordan Hill, Oxford OX2 8EJ
a division of Reed Educational & Professional Publishing Ltd
OXFORD   MELBOURNE   AUCKLAND
JOHANNESBURG   BLANTYRE   GABORONE
IBADAN   PORTSMOUTH (NH) USA   CHICAGO

First published in Great Britain by Methuen Children's Books Ltd 1984

First published in the New Windmill Series 1995

99 10 9 8 7 6 5

ISBN 0 435 12434 X

British Library Cataloguing in Publication Data
for this title is available from the British Library

Typeset by CentraCet Limited, Cambridge
Printed in England by Clays Ltd, St Ives plc

*To Daisy and John*

# Contents

# 1  The Sea Bride

The moment I saw her, I wanted her. She was standing on the pavement outside Willoughby's, staring over my head with her bold black eyes. Nothing warned me. No cloud suddenly darkened the sky. No wind blew coldly down my neck. I thought she was beautiful.

My father and I are hunters. Bargain hunters. Walter Muffat, Antiques, that's us. Or rather that's my father. When I'm grown up, I'm going to be "& SON" in gold letters over our shop. At the moment, I'm only Sam Muffat, Oddments.

During the school holidays, I have a stall in the paved yard beside our shop. A hand-painted notice says: SAM MUFFAT. ODDMENTS. BARGAINS. IF YOU CAN'T AFFORD ANYTHING INSIDE, TRY ME.

My mother disapproved. She said it looked cheap. But my father just laughed.

"Everyone has to begin small," he said. "Sam's doing all right. You can't start too young at this game."

For I was only twelve, just twelve; it was my birthday. I felt rich and lucky, setting out for

1

Willoughby's Sale Rooms with my father. I had thirty-eight pounds in my pocket, part birthday money and part savings, and I was going to buy the bargain that would make my fortune. Or so I thought.

But Willoughby's was far grander than the local auctions I was used to. Far grander than the sales, (jumble and church bazaar) where I normally bought things for my stall. It was crowded with dealers from London, who nodded to my father, glanced at me briefly, and then talked above my head as if I was not there. I wanted to tell them that I was a dealer like themselves, but I seemed to have lost my voice.

There were not enough chairs and, being only a boy, I did not get one. I perched on the edge of a table, (Victorian, mahogany, one leg repaired) until a porter shooed me off. Then I sat on a windowsill so sharp and narrow that I feared it would slice me in two. As I watched and listened, the money in my pocket seemed to shrivel. My father had warned me. "Thirty-eight pounds won't go far at Willoughby's," he'd said. He was right.

"Who'll start me at a hundred?" the auctioneer asked. "I'm offered a hundred. A hundred and ten. A hundred and twenty. A hundred and forty. Any advance on a hundred and forty?"

I began to think I'd never get a chance to make a bid.

Then one of the porters held up a china shepherdess, complete with sheep. (Staffordshire, circa 1875.)

"What am I bid for this? Who'll start me at twenty pounds?"

I still could not find my voice, but that didn't worry me. Many dealers just signal to the auctioneer by raising their catalogues or nodding their heads. There is a joke that if you sneeze at an auction, you may find you have bought a grand piano by mistake. It isn't true. I could have had hay fever and the auctioneer wouldn't have cared. He saw me raise my catalogue. I know he did! He looked straight at me. His glance travelled from my head to my toes and back again, (not a long journey: I'm small for my age). Then he ignored me and took the bid from a fat woman in a green coat.

"Twenty pounds I'm bid. Twenty-two. Twenty-four. Twenty-six. Any advance on twenty-six?"

This time I waved my catalogue so vigorously that I nearly fell off the windowsill. He noticed me then all right.

"I'm not sure if the young gentleman over there is bidding," he said. "Or swatting a fly."

Everyone laughed and turned to look at me. My face went crimson. I hated them. I mumbled something inaudible, slid off the windowsill and tried, unsuccessfully, to sink through the floor.

"My son was bidding," my father said, annoyed on my behalf. "Twenty-eight pounds you're bid, sir."

3

The fat woman in the green coat smiled at me nastily.

"Thirty," she said.

It went for thirty-six pounds, and not to me. I didn't want it any longer. I didn't want anything in that beastly sale room. I was no longer certain I wanted to be "& SON" in gold letters over our shop door.

My father glanced at me, worried that I was disappointed with my birthday treat. He is a very nice man, my father. So I smiled at him and whispered, "Well I broke the ice, didn't I? Talking of ice, I think I'll pop out for a lolly. Back in half-an-hour." I waved my hand jauntily, trying not to look like someone who'd had his first bid ignored and his second made fun of.

So that is how I came to be outside Willoughby's, cooling my hot cheeks in the fresh air, when they unloaded her from the van and placed her carefully on the pavement. For my black-eyed beauty was a ship's figurehead. She was leaning forward as if breasting the waves. Her hair, black and glossy with paint, streamed back over her shoulders. Her cheeks were pink, her skin white, and her breasts, as big as water melons, seemed about to burst out of her sea-green dress. She had, of course, no feet. A heavy iron stand supported her, otherwise she'd have fallen flat on her nose.

They could keep their simpering china shepherdesses. I wanted this stern beauty, (for she was not smiling). Her black eyes, fixed so intently

4

on a faraway horizon, seemed to reflect wonders I could not see; strange islands, flying fish, great white whales ... She had about her the very smell of the sea, and glistened in the bright paint as if still wet. A shop awning, flapping in the breeze, sounded like a galleon in full sail. The paving stones seemed to tilt beneath my feet, as if the town was suddenly afloat. I wanted her. I wanted her in our yard, between my stall and the tub of scarlet geraniums, attracting the eye of every rich customer who strolled by. But I did not think I could afford her.

The dealer who owned her, (H. Wiggins & Son it said on the side of his van) was arguing with one of the porters from Willoughby's.

"We can't possibly get her in before the 17th, sir," the porter was saying.

"That's no good. Today. It must be today. Surely you can slip her in at the end ..."

"I'm sorry, sir. We're running late as it is," the porter said.

"I could make it worth your while," the man suggested, clinking some money in his pocket. But the porter was not interested. I knew him. His name was Alf and he had a girlfriend who worked in Boots. Perhaps he was taking her out that night. Perhaps it was *his* birthday.

"We can store her for you, sir," he suggested.

H. Wiggins looked doubtful.

"I'm going away today. I wanted to be rid ... I wanted her off my hands."

As they talked, I was walking round my

beauty, examining her with a connoisseur's eye. The paint, which had looked fresh and new from a distance, now revealed cracks through which you could see the wood. It was old, but sound. Oak, I thought, very dark; weathered. I put my hand out . . .

"Don't touch!" said a young man sharply. He had been leaning against the van, a thin figure in faded jeans and a tattered jersey – "& Son", I thought.

"He's trade," Alf said, nodding towards me, "Walter Muffat, Antiques. Son of. Perhaps you can do a private deal." He winked at me and hurried back into the auction rooms.

H. Wiggins & Son looked at me thoughtfully.

"Trade, eh?" said the older man, "Is your dad inside?" He jerked his thumb towards Willoughby's.

I shook my head. It wasn't really a lie. I mean, I didn't actually say "no." I was just shaking the hair out of my eyes. I couldn't help it if they misunderstood me.

"I might be interested, if the price is right," I said. "I'm a dealer."

I waited for them to laugh; people usually do when I say this, but not H. Wiggins & Son. If anything, they looked sad. Their faces were pale and weary. Their dark eyes surveyed me seriously, with a kind of gloomy hope.

I suppose it should have warned me, but I was enjoying myself at last. I strutted round the figurehead, peering closely at the paint, ran my fingers gently down her arm, rapped her with my knuckles, as if by doing so, I could immediately tell if she were wormy or cracked.

"Sound as a bell," the older man said.

"She's been repainted," I said sternly, for the paint, though cracked, could not have been the original.

"Restored," he countered.

"Hmm-mm," I stroked my chin with my thumb, just as my father did when he was pretending to be doubtful.

"Where's she from?" I asked next.

"Newcastle. Off a Victorian frigate. *The Sea Bride*, it was – sailed the East India run in her day. *The Sea Bride*, now there's a pretty name for her." He raised his hand as if to slap her bottom, but thought better of it and put his hand in his pocket. "And a right buxom beauty she is too," he said, staring at her.

His expression puzzled me. There was no admiration in it, whatever he might say. He looked almost as if he hated her. But I, with thirty-eight pounds in my pocket, and my head filled with sailing-ships on bright seas, heard no warning bell.

"What are you asking for her?" I said.

They closed in, one on either side of me. I felt very small between them.

"Make me an offer," H. Wiggins said.

I did not want to. I was afraid they would laugh when they heard how little I had to give.

For I thought she was worth at least two hundred pounds.

I stepped back. Shrugged. Shook my head slowly. They watched me.

"Business is bad," I said.

And they nodded most eagerly.

"People are not buying, not things like this," I gestured at the figurehead.

Now they were shaking their heads. "No. Things are very slow," they agreed. "Money's tight. You'd not find a buyer easy for her."

I was disconcerted. They seemed to be on my side. This was not the way bargaining was usually done.

"Come on, young sir," the father said, "for a quick sale, I'm prepared to let her go cheap. Dirt cheap. Don't be shy. Make me an offer. I'll not laugh, however small it is."

"Twenty-five pounds," I said, and my voice squeaked with embarrassment.

But they did not laugh. They exchanged unreadable glances.

Then the father said, "Fifty."

I was astonished. Only fifty pounds? My heart began to race. I tried not to look excited, but I could feel my cheeks flushing.

"Thirty," I said.

"Oh, you're in luck, young sir. I'm in a generous mood today. Forty pounds – and not a penny less."

So near. So nearly mine.

"Thirty-five." Now my voice was hoarse, "thirty-five – and not a penny more."

"*Done!*" H. Wiggins spoke so quickly that his mouth opened and shut like a trap. "It's a bargain."

He held out his hand and I shook it. Then, finding he was still holding it out, I counted the money into it with shaking fingers. He gave me a receipt, stuffed the money carelessly into his pocket, and smiled for the first time.

"You drive a hard bargain, son of Walter Muffat, Antiques," he said. "You're too sharp for an old fellow like me. She's yours, young sir. Not mine any longer. All yours." His eyes seemed full of a secret glee. "And may you have better luck with her than I had."

He climbed into his van. I heard the engine start.

His son still lingered on the pavement. He looked ill. His eyes, in his thin face, were reddened, with dark smudges under them, as if he had not slept for many nights.

He came up close to me and said in a low voice, "Keep her out of doors. Don't bring her into the shop. Don't let her into the house."

I must have looked surprised because he added quickly, "She'll come to no harm. Not her. Rain and sleet, hail and wind, they'll not hurt *her*. Leave her outside, and . . ." here his voice sank to a whisper, "and shut your windows at night."

Then he too jumped into the van, and it disappeared down the street in a cloud of exhaust. I

9

stood on the pavement, staring after them in astonishment. My father, coming out of Willoughby's to look for me, laughed when he saw me there. He said I looked bewitched. He said I was rocking on my feet, as if I were all at sea.

We put the Sea Bride in the yard, beside the tub of scarlet geraniums. I wished the sun had not gone in. I wanted her to look her best.

"I don't like her," my sister said. Becky is only seven, and very silly.

But my mother was impressed.

"Thirty-five pounds!" she exclaimed. "You're joking! There must be something wrong." (This is high praise from my mother. She never trusts bargains if they seem too good. Dad says that when he offered her his hand and heart, she examined them under a magnifying glass for hidden flaws.) "Did he give you a receipt?"

"Yes." I handed it to her.

"H. Wiggins & Son, Portsmouth. Never heard of them. Have you, Walter?"

My father shook his head. "Lots of dealers I haven't heard of," he said cheerfully. But he too looked puzzled. "What was the man thinking of? He could have got a couple of hundred for her in any sale room."

"Perhaps he didn't like her," Becky said. "Perhaps he didn't like the way she stares."

"Do you think she's a fake, Dad?" I asked anxiously.

"She looks genuine enough to me. Not that I'm

an expert. Not my line. I'll get old Watson to have a look at her. Don't worry, Sam. She's well worth the money, even if they knocked her up in their own back yard. She's a handsome lass. The Sea Bride, eh? Mrs Neptune herself. I hope her old man doesn't come and fetch her away."

"What old man?" Becky asked.

"Father Neptune," I explained. You always have to explain jokes to Becky.

"Who's he?"

"The sea god."

"Why'd he want her?"

"She's his bride. The Sea Bride, see?"

"The She Bride?"

Becky could go on like this for hours.

"Oh, shut up!" I said.

"Your Mrs Neptune's a haughty young madam, isn't she?" my mother said. "Looks as if she didn't think our yard was good enough for her."

"Don't you like her, Mum?"

"Oh, . . . yes. Yes, dear, of course," she said doubtfully.

"I don't! She's horrible!" Becky said. "I hate her!"

What was the matter with them? Then I thought, catching sight of a smudge of chocolate icing on Becky's cheek, it's my birthday. That's the trouble. Other people's birthdays go on too long.

I took pity on them. "What's for tea?" I asked.

Becky beamed happily.

"Sea biscuits and salt water! Sea biscuits and

11

salt water!" she chanted shrilly, and shrieked with laughter.

Funny. We are thirty miles or more from the nearest coast, yet I fancied, for a moment, that I could smell salt water. And I did not want to go into the house and eat sausages and peanuts, sandwiches and candled cake. I wanted to stay in the yard, where the cool breeze seemed to carry the tang of the faraway sea. I glanced back. She looked lonely, my black-eyed beauty. Leaning forward, she strained against her iron stand, as if she wanted to get away.

There was a high wind in the night. Though I slept through it, its wailing must have invaded my dreams. I had a nightmare, but I cannot remember what it was about. I woke, carrying only the terror with me from my sleep. Becky was in my room.

"Sam! Wake up, Sam!" she cried. "Your Mrs Neptune's got away!"

I leapt out of bed and ran to the window. In the yard below, there were broken tiles on the paving-stones. The dustbins had blown over and scattered their rubbish everywhere. A branch had broken off the silver birch. Then I saw her. She had fallen across our wrought-iron gates and was leaning out into the street.

"Sam!" called my father, catching sight of me at the window. "Come and help!"

"How did she get there?"

"Dunno. Must have blown, I suppose. Funny. You'd have thought she'd have fallen over before she reached the gates. Lucky we shut them at night or there's no telling where she'd have gone."

She was heavy and part of her stand had got caught in one of the decorative loops of the gates. My father could not lift her by himself. I dressed quickly and went to help him. Seen so close, her eyes were as black and shiny as tar. She gazed down the hill so eagerly; it was hard to believe she wasn't looking at something, something too far away for me to see. It wasn't the road to the coast. That was at the back of our house.

"If you went on and on that way, as far as you could," I said, pointing, "where would you get to, Dad?"

"Ease her back a little, Sam. A bit more," my father said. "Steady now. Up she rises . . ."

She was heavy. "Dad," I panted, "where would you get to, if . . ."

"I heard you the first time. (Steady now! Careful does it!) Why, I suppose you'd come to the sea in the end. We're on an island. Whichever way you go, you'd come to the sea in the end."

My poor Sea Bride. That afternoon, my father bolted her iron stand to the wall behind her.

"We don't want her running off again," he said. "That should hold her."

I thought she looked angry. I swept and tidied our yard, and weeded the tubs of scarlet geraniums. If I thought to appease her, it did not work. That night, water somehow got into our shop, staining the polished top of a Sheraton table and soaking the set of tapestry chairs.

"Where's it come from?" my father demanded angrily. He looked upwards, almost as if he were reproaching God. There were no damp patches on the ceiling.

"Did you leave a window open?" my mother asked.

"Of course not!"

"Perhaps it came down the chimney," I suggested.

"Don't be so stupid, Sam!" he shouted.

I flushed and went out, ignoring the apology he called after me. Becky followed me into the yard.

"It's her," she whispered. "*She* did it."

"Don't be so stupid," I said, thinking I might as well pass it on.

"She did! She did! She's a sea witch!" Becky said. "I hate her!"

She stood in front of Mrs Neptune and put out her tongue. Then suddenly she looked scared. She ran over to me and took hold of my hand. She really is very silly at times.

"She can't hurt you," I said comfortingly. I reached out and tapped the white wooden arm: "She's not real."

"Touch wood! You're touching wood!" Becky cried, and giggled.

The Sea Bride stared over our heads with her bold black eyes. The sun came out, and a small wind stirred in the ivy. Again I seemed to smell

14

the salt tang of the sea, as if it were a perfume she wore.

"Who's she looking for?" Becky whispered. "Who does she keep looking for?"

I woke early next morning. It must have poured in the night. I had not shut my window and the curtains were soaked. There was a dark wet stain on the carpet like blood. The dye had run from my new slippers: when I picked them up, my hands were red.

I stared out of the window. In the yard below, Mrs Neptune stood, glittering wet in the morning light. How beautiful she looked. Almost alive. I could have sworn a strand of her hair moved gently in the wind.

I dressed quickly and went outside. Puddles of water lay in the hollows of the paving and little stones, grey and brown, were scattered everywhere. As I walked, I looked round, puzzled. Then I stepped on something soft and fleshy, like a fat man's hand. I snatched my foot back.

It was a fish, dead; its round eye glazed, its silver skin striped with black. A mackerel.

I picked it up. It was quite stiff. At first I thought our cat had been raiding the larder. Then I noticed there were more of them, floating in puddles, caught up in the ivy, half-hidden among the red geraniums. There must have been twenty, at least.

I gathered them into an old bucket and hid them in the shed. I don't know why. They made

15

me uneasy, somehow. Then I swept up the shingle and hid it behind the dustbins. My mother came out as I was putting the broom away.

"You're up early, Sam. Tidying up again for Mrs Neptune, I see. Well, she doesn't seem to have suffered in the storm last night."

"Rain and sleet, hail and wind, they won't hurt her," I said.

Mum looked surprised. "Is that from a poem?" she asked. "Well, she may be weatherproof, but if you ask me, it was just as well Dad bolted her stand to the wall. She might have fallen over and cracked. Breakfast in ten minutes, Sam."

"It's not mackerel, is it, Mum?"

"No. Why, did you fancy one? I could get you one for your tea, if you like."

"No. I don't like fish."

She looked at me, then shook her head, smiling. "Kids!" she said, and went back into the house.

I went into the shed, took the fish out of the bucket and wrapped them in an old piece of sacking. Then I went out through the yard gate, walked quickly down the street and put my bundle into old Mrs Rutherford's dustbin, pushing it well down till it was hidden beneath the eggshells and tea leaves.

On my way back, running through our yard, I slipped on something and fell, grazing the skin off my knees. A piece of weed had brought me down. I peeled it off my sandal. Dark brown it was, and rubbery, covered with little blisters that popped between my fingers. Seaweed. It stank of the sea. How did it get there? How did the fish and shingle get there? I did not know. We are thirty miles from the nearest coast.

"Why are you lying down?" It was my sister, still in her nightgown, her bare feet paddling in a puddle. "Did she knock you over?"

"Who?"

"Her. Mrs Neptune."

"Don't be silly," I said, picking myself up. "She's not real. She's only made of wood."

Becky said nothing. She was sucking the sleeve of her nightie, and looking sly.

"Why don't you like her?" I asked curiously.

At first I thought she was not going to tell me. Then she came over, caught hold of my ear and pulled my head down to her level.

"She doesn't like you," she whispered.

I was hurt. It's silly, I know, but somehow it hurt me. I looked at Mrs Neptune. I still thought she was beautiful. As ever, her black eyes stared over my head. Leaning forward on her stand, she looked eager, expectant; as if she were waiting for someone. But not for me.

That night I shut my window. My mother, coming into my room to kiss me goodnight, complained that it was like an oven.

"Why have you shut your window, Sam? You'll never sleep in this heat."

"Don't open it, Mum! Leave it! Please."

She looked at me in surprise.

"It's going to rain tonight," I said.

"A little rain won't hurt. Better than baking." She opened the window about six inches from the top. "There," she said.

As soon as she had gone downstairs, I shut it again. Then I tiptoed into Becky's room next door. She was asleep, clutching her teddy bear. Gently, slowly, I closed her window. She did not stir.

When I woke up, it was dark. My bed was rocking. Water crashed against the window. Wind screamed down the chimney. The whole house shuddered and swayed about me. Something crashed downstairs. My light would not work.

I heard my sister scream. Footsteps ran along the passage to her room. I heard my mother's voice.

I was out of bed. I crossed the heaving floor to the window and looked out. It was all black and banging outside. Then lightning lit the sky. Down below, I saw the Sea Bride. White birds screamed about her head. She was leaning into the wind and the waves. She looked huge, alive, triumphant. Great grey mountains of water swirled about her. I saw some dark wood smash against the wall of our house. A piece of wrecked ship? Our garden bench? I did not know. It was all dark again.

I leaned against the windowsill and felt it crack and quiver. I heard my father shout downstairs, and my sister screamed again.

I opened my window wide. Water smashed into my face, soaking me, blinding me, salt on my lips. I clung to the windowsill and screamed into the dark.

"Stop it! Stop it! I'll let her go! I promise I'll let her go!"

There must have been another flash of lightning. I saw a huge, green, translucent wave coming for me. I thought it had a face. Dark whirlpools were its eyes, wild hair and beard like a waterfall streamed over its cheeks and chin. Then the water held me, shook me, curled round me and tried to suck me out into the wild night. My fingers scrabbled at the windowsill – and slipped.

Now my father's arms were round me. He threw me across the room on to my bed and slammed the window shut.

"Tell him I'll give her back!" I screamed. Then I must have fainted.

"Terrible storm, wasn't it?" my mother said.

It was five in the morning. We were sitting on damp chairs in the damp kitchen, drinking tea. Outside, everything was quiet. No-one answered her. We did not know what to say.

The silence seemed to worry her.

"Never known anything like it. If you ask me, it's all these atom bombs. It's not natural."

"No," said my father. Then he put down his cup and looked at me. "Better get going. Are you sure you still want to do it, Sam?"

"Yes."

"Walter, it's silly," my mother said uneasily, "throwing away good money."

"Don't stop them, Mum! Don't! Please don't!" Becky cried, and began to whimper. Mum put her arm round her and was silent.

My father and I went out into the yard. It was littered with debris. Our garden bench was in pieces. Broken tiles were scattered on the wet paving. The geraniums had lost all their petals, which lay like drops of blood among the broken glass.

Only the Sea Bride was undamaged. Bolted to the wall, she still stared over our heads with her round black eyes.

My father had brought out a wrench and a screwdriver. We unfastened her from her iron stand and carried her out to our van. Thirty miles through the quiet, grey morning we drove, umtil we reached the shore. Even without her stand, she was heavy. We put her on our trolley and dragged it over the shingle to an old wall that ran into the sea like a stone finger. There was no-one about. We wheeled the trolley along the wide flat top of the wall. The sea had been quiet when we came, but now little waves ran out to greet us. They lapped at our feet, like small wet hands hurrying us along.

"Careful, Sam," my father said. "It's slippery."

There were larger waves now. As we neared the end of the wall, we could see them hurrying over the smooth surface of the sea. There was one behind them, a great green mountain, capped with a crest of snow.

"Good God!" my father cried, and grabbed my arm.

But they did not swamp us. Instead they seemed to hold back, rearing up from the body of the sea in peaks of foam.

"Quick!"

We picked up the Sea Bride between us, and threw her into the sea. A wave rushed to meet her, lifted her on high and spun her round. Now she was facing us. White spray dimmed her black hair like a bridal veil. As she sank, her eyes, at last on my level, gazed straight into mine. I thought she smiled. Then the wave spun her round again and carried her swiftly out to sea. We watched until she was a mere speck, skimming the green water.

# 2 Patchwork

The tall red-brick house cast a long shadow over the lane. There was grass growing in its gravel drive, and dandelions among the neglected roses. Behind one of the dusty windows, an old lady could be seen dimly. Sometimes she would be gazing out as if expecting someone to come. Sometimes her head would be bent over her sewing, as if she had given up hope. Her name was Mrs Drummond, and she had three horrible daughters.

Horrible. It was the only word for them. They had been greedy children, Aunt Sarah told me, cold-hearted and arrogant, taking all they could get, and demanding more. Now their mother was old and poor, her husband dead, money and servants all gone, they never came near her.

Grey as a ghost, the old lady sat by her window all day, sewing her patchwork quilts. Meanwhile the house crumbled about her. Tiles blew off the roof, plaster fell from the ceilings; and still the old lady waited in vain.

* * *

It made Aunt Sarah mad.

"Those horrible daughters," she said. "I could wring their necks."

I smiled. Aunt Sarah, trying to sound fierce, was like a dove growling: she fooled no-one. Certainly not me. I had been coming to stay with her every summer for the last four years, and knew her too well.

"I bet if they do come, you'll just offer them a cup of tea," I said.

"Not me. I wouldn't give them good morning."

"Bet you would."

"Ten pence," Aunt Sarah said promptly. "Though it's a shame to rob a child."

"Do you think they ever will come?" I asked hopefully. I wanted to see them for myself, these monstrous daughters I had heard so much about. I think I half imagined them with claws like vultures and snouts like pigs.

Aunt Sarah shook her head. "No," she said. "Your money's safe. They'll never come now. That poor old lady. I'm sure she doesn't eat enough." She looked round her kitchen thoughtfully. It was difficult. Mrs Drummond was proud, and hated to accept help she could not pay for. Little as she had, she always wanted to give something in return. "Here, take her this, Kate," Aunt Sarah said, handing me a basket of her best apples, picked fresh from the tree that morning. "Tell her they're windfalls and would only rot if left. And mind, don't let her give you anything."

"I won't," I promised.

23

The old lady was pleased to see me. She accepted the apples and offered me a glass of milk. Remembering Aunt Sarah's warning, I said I was dieting, and would rather have water. I refused a biscuit, and a chocolate, but stayed to chat with her. I loved watching the old lady sew. Though her fingers were freckled with age, the needle flew in and out like a silver dart, and the quilt blossomed in her hands, pale and bright, like a miraculous flower in the dusty room.

I think she saw the admiration in my eyes, for she smiled.

"I must show you my masterpiece," she said.

She took a bundle of cloth out of a drawer, and unfolding it, spread it over the carpet.

I stared at it in wonder. I had never seen anything like it. In the centre of the quilt, there were strange trees and stranger animals; white damask unicorns, lions striped like tigers, dogs with tasselled tails, birds with flowered feathers and purple-spotted snakes. It was a quilt fit for a dreamer of fine dreams, and I loved it.

"It's beautiful," I said. "Oh, Mrs Drummond, it's beautiful!"

The old lady smiled with pleasure at my praise.

"I'd like you to have it," she said, folding it up.

Hot with embarrassment, I stammered, "I can't ... I didn't mean ... It's much too good! Honest, Mrs Drummond, I couldn't take it."

"Then I'll leave it to you in my will," the old

24

lady said. "I *want* you to have it. You are a kind child."

Aunt Sarah, when I told her this, laughed and said, "Well, I hope she remembers. I'd hate those daughters to get it. I'm not usually a spiteful woman, but when I think of the way they've treated their mother, I wish, I just wish something would happen to take them down a peg or two."

The following summer, old Mrs Drummond died. She passed away quietly in her sleep, Aunt Sarah wrote. It was a peaceful end.

I was sorry. I had liked the old lady. But I could not help remembering the animal quilt, and wondering if it was now mine. I did not say anything about it, however, not wanting to be thought as greedy as Mrs Drummond's daughters.

"Do you think I ought to go down for the funeral?" I asked my mother.

She shook her head.

"It's not as if you're a relative," she said. "Funerals are depressing things, even when it's the old that die. You go down on Sunday as arranged. Aunt Sarah's looking forward to seeing you. She'll be missing the old lady, and a young, noisy, bouncing girl like you will take her mind off it."

I was not altogether flattered by this description, but I let it pass.

"I wonder if Mrs Drummond's daughters will be there," I said.

"You'll soon find out," my mother said.

The tall red house looked more neglected than ever. The windows were shut. No face looked out through the dusty glass. As I passed it, I thought for a moment that I heard odd sounds; shrieks of terror, running feet and shrill laughter. But when I looked up and down the lane, I could see no-one. I walked on, puzzled.

Later, when we were sitting in the garden, I asked Aunt Sarah if there was anyone staying in the house next door.

"No," she said. "It's empty now."

"Didn't her daughters come, then?"

"They came," Aunt Sarah said grimly. "Oh yes, they managed to tear themselves away from their grand parties long enough to see their mother buried. Kept looking at their watches all through the service. D'you know what I heard one of them tell the vicar? That it had happened at a most inconvenient time! *Inconvenient*! What did they expect the poor old lady to do? Write and ask their permission – please may I die today or would you rather I left it till next week? Horrible creatures, I could've hit them!"

"Won't they be coming back?" I asked, disappointed, for I had wanted to see them just once.

"Yes. Next Wednesday," Aunt Sarah told me. "They want to sort out their mother's things before the house is put up for sale. They're staying the night, before driving off to some grand house party or other."

"Husbands and all?"

"No. I expect the poor men are far too busy making money. It'll just be those three idle women."

"I hope their beds are damp! I hope the ceilings fall down on their heads!" I cried.

To my surprise, Aunt Sarah, who had often wished far worse things on Mrs Drummond's daughters, looked embarrassed.

"It was a bit awkward," she said, not meeting my eye. "The vicar introduced me to them, saying what a help I'd been to their mother – you know the silly way he goes on. I think they took me for the cleaning lady, (as if she could've afforded one, poor old soul)! Anyway, they asked me if I'd air the house and make up the beds for them . . ."

"What cheek! I hope you told them to go to hell."

"Now, Kate, how could I? With the vicar standing right there, saying what a good woman I was. And me without a word on my tongue fit for his ears. I didn't say anything, though I suppose I might have just nodded . . ."

"*Aunt Sarah!*"

"It's the old lady I'm doing it for," my aunt said defensively. "She wouldn't have wanted her rich daughters to know how poorly she lived. Stuck-up bitches that they are!"

"Did you offer them tea?" I asked, remembering our bet.

Aunt Sarah looked shifty.

"Come on. Own up," I said.

Aunt Sarah sighed, and taking a ten pence piece from her pocket, gave it to me.

I laughed. "Never mind," I said. "I'll help you clean up the place tomorrow." I thought for a moment. "Snails in their beds?" I suggested hopefully.

"That would be unkind," Aunt Sarah said. "Poor snails. They might suffocate. No, seriously, Kate, no tricks. Promise?"

"Oh, all right," I said. "But I wish . . ." I stopped abruptly. For I seemed to hear again strange sounds; shrieks of terror, running feet and shrill laughter. But when I looked into the lane, there was no-one there.

On Monday, we let ourselves into Mrs Drummond's house, flung open the dusty windows to let in the summer air, and swept and dusted and polished until everything shone. In one of the spare bedrooms, beneath a dust sheet, we found the animal quilt. It glowed richly in the sunlight, like a stained glass window.

We bent over it.

"There's a bit of the dress I wore to Clare's wedding," Aunt Sarah said, pointing, "and that's from the one I made for your school play, remember?"

"Yes. And that's the green one I wore to the Johnson's party, when Timmy kissed me behind the door, soppy drip! And look, isn't that one of Mum's?"

"Yes. And I remember that ... and that ... Why, Kate, there's our lives sewn into that quilt. She's saved up all the bits and pieces I've given her over the years, and made this beautiful thing of them. It's fit to go in a museum." She caught sight of my face then. I must have been looking hopeful, because she shook her head, and said ruefully: "No, I doubt if it'll come to you now, Kate. They say the old lady left no will."

I was bitterly disappointed.

"She wanted me to have it!" I said. "Can't we just take it?"

Aunt Sarah was shocked. "That wouldn't be right," she said, touching the quilt gently. "I'd like you to have it, but unless she put something in a letter, well, I can't see those daughters giving anything away. Not them! They wouldn't part with an empty crisp bag."

In this she did them an injustice. They arrived on Wednesday, sweeping up the drive in a huge glittering car from which they emerged like three bears, fat in their fur coats. It was a warm day and they must have been far too hot. It was probably this that made their faces so red, and not my hostile stare. I had promised Aunt Sarah not to be rude, and I wasn't going to be. I wasn't going to say a word. But remembering poor old Mrs Drummond, I could not bring myself to smile.

They asked us to help them carry their cases

29

into the house. There were a surprising number of these, all heavy.

"Are you staying more than the one night?" Aunt Sarah asked, puzzled, but was told that they were going on the next day to stay with an old friend of theirs, and that was why there was so much luggage.

"Dear Lady Bridlington" one of them said, flashing the title at us like a diamond ring. "She does so miss her bridge when she's in the country. She's always begging us to come down. We felt we simply had to take pity on her."

Pity? I thought, what do you know about pity, you old bag?

"Can't you leave some of the cases in the car?" I asked, for my arms were aching. I got a cold look from the largest of the daughters, a massive woman, with chins enough for the three of them. Her name was Mabel Platt.

"We have a lot of valuables with us," she told me. "I shall feel safer if they're in the house. You look a strong girl. Surely you don't mind carrying a few cases?"

Conscious of Aunt Sarah's eyes on me, I said nothing.

When the last case had been carried into the hall, the three women looked round critically. If they noticed how bright and shining the house was, they did not say so, but took it all for granted. They did not offer us tea.

"Thank you, Mrs – er – Perkins. We mustn't take up any more of your time," Mrs Platt said

30

to Aunt Sarah, as if she were dismissing a servant: "Oh, by the way, if there's any little thing you'd like to remember our mother by . . .?"

I looked quickly, pleadingly at Aunt Sarah.

"Well," she said, embarrassed, "I'd not be asking for myself. But there's a patchwork quilt in one of the bedrooms . . ."

The woman raised her eyebrows. "Ah, Mother's famous quilts," she said, and gave a nasty little laugh. "No, I'm afraid I didn't mean anything quite so . . . well, to be frank, quite on that scale . . ."

"She said she'd leave it to me in her will!" I burst out.

Three cold pairs of eyes turned on me.

"My mother did not make a will," Mrs Platt said. "And I'm afraid we can't really be expected to give away her things just on somebody's say so. After all, anyone could claim . . ."

"She did say she wanted me to have it! She did!"

"Mother was always so foolishly generous," Mrs Platt said. "I'm afraid she often promised things, and then forgot all about them."

"Anyone could get round her," another daughter said.

"I'm sure she must have meant us to have it," said the third. "After all, we are her . . ." She stopped.

From somewhere in the house, an odd noise was coming. High-pitched, sharp, repetitive.

Like the licking of a steel tongue against steel teeth.

"What's that?" Mrs Platt asked. We all listened, but it had stopped and did not come again. "Oh, well," she said, and shrugged. "Now where was I?"

"Not here!" I shouted, remembering the pale face gazing out through the dusty glass, day after day, waiting in vain. "Not when she needed you!"

Aunt Sarah bustled me out of the house.

"Now you're not to be talking to me, Kate," she said. "Or I'll say something I shouldn't. Of all the ... I'd like to ... well, never you mind. I'm glad you said what you did. They had it coming. I'll not set foot in the house again, though they beg me to on their bended knees. I'd kick their teeth in sooner!"

But we did go back. The next morning, there was an angry knocking at the door. Mrs Platt stood outside. Her face was patched with red. Her descending chins shook with rage.

"Come with me! Come with me this minute. I have something to show you," she said, and marched down the path without looking to see if we followed. Aunt Sarah stared after her in bewilderment, then looked at me.

"What's all that about?" she asked.

"Let's go and see."

Aunt Sarah hesitated. But she was as curious as I was. "Might as well. I forgot to give them their key back yesterday. They'll be wanting that," she said, as if in excuse.

So we followed the fat woman into the house next door. There were open suitcases all over the floor. The other two daughters were kneeling in front of them, holding up what appeared to be silken nets, that swayed and glimmered in the light.

"Look! Look what she's done to our dresses!" they said, and the tears they had not shed for their mother now spilled out of their eyes.

The dresses were ruined. Out of the rich material, little squares and hexagons and diamonds and triangles had been cut. All that was left was a web of gleaming threads, on which a few buttons sat like spiders.

"Why, whoever did that?" Aunt Sarah exclaimed in innocent amazement.

Their eyes turned on me. Their fingers pointed.

"Her!" they said. "She did it out of spite, because we wouldn't let her have that quilt."

I stood there, my face flushing, unable to speak. I knew I must look the very picture of guilt.

"Who else could have done it?" they demanded, when Aunt Sarah protested. "Unless you did it yourself. No-one else had a key."

"No!" I said hopelessly. "It wasn't! It wasn't me!".

I could see the disbelief on their faces. Even Aunt Sarah was looking at me with a worried question in her eyes.

33

"I didn't! I didn't do it!" I said, trying not to cry.

Then it came again, the odd metallic sound, cold and quick and inhuman, like handcuffs chattering together. I was frightened. I thought the police were waiting outside the door.

"It wasn't me!" I shouted.

The others did not seem to have noticed the noise.

"My dresses! My best dresses!" the youngest daughter mourned. "What am I going to wear to the Hunt Ball? What am I going to wear to Lady Bardolph's party?"

"You're going to pay for this," the middle daughter said, glaring at me.

Then they heard it. They all heard it. A shrill, snapping sound, wheeze click, wheeze click, wheeze click, like metal teeth chewing through iron bars.

We turned and stared. Like silver birds of prey, a flock of scissors flew in through the open door, large ones, small ones, straight ones, curved ones, all with cruel pointed beaks. The screws that held their blades together glittered like angry eyes.

Round and round, they wheeled and darted, with their strange discordant cry. Then suddenly they swooped towards the three fat, terrified daughters. The women screamed and flung up their arms to protect their faces from the fierce beaks. Watching in horror, I expected to see blood spring from the plump, pampered flesh.

34

But the scissor birds were after different prey. As the women ran this way and that, squealing like pigs, little squares of silk were cut from the very dresses they wore, fluttering down to the carpet like petals from a bunch of summer roses.

Screaming, the three daughters rushed from the house. We stared after them. Down the path they ran, with the scissors pecking and snipping their clothes, scattering the bright silk like confetti in the wind. Down the lane they ran, three fat, pink, naked ladies, now as bare as the day they were born. And the scissor birds flew up into the sky, singing a thin silver song of triumph. Then they vanished.

"Well I never!" Aunt Sarah said, looking at me in amazement. Then we clung together, and began laughing hysterically. The sound of our shrill laughter followed the shrieking women as they ran down the lane.

Mrs Rogers, at the corner house, took pity on Mrs Drummond's daughters.

"I found them in my garden all dressed up in togas, like them Romans in plays," she told us later that morning. "'And that's my best table-cloth you're wearing,' I said, for hadn't I embroidered it with my own hand? 'And that's gran's linen sheets!' Helped themselves as cool as you please from my washing line. Though I had to laugh. 'And what were you doing running about stark naked in a respectable woman's garden, I'd

35

like to know?' I said. Well! You'll never believe the tale they told."

"No," Aunt Sarah said, smiling ruefully at me. "I don't suppose anybody ever will. Not even seeing it with their own eyes."

"Been at the bottle, if you ask me, and it not half-past ten in the morning! From London they are, and we all know what they get up to there. Well, what I've come about, they've asked me to load up their car and drive it round. Then they're off, though whether they're fit to drive is another matter. I'm to lock up next door. Never want to see the house again, they said, though I'm sure I don't know why."

"I'll give you the key," Aunt Sarah said.

"Thanks. Oh yes, and they said young Kate here was to have the patchwork quilt she wanted. I was to tell you their mother had written last year, saying she was to have it. They said you'd know the one."

I looked at Aunt Sarah, who smiled.

"Yes, take it, Kate," she said. "The old lady wanted you to have it. No-one can doubt that now."

Joyfully I went running off to fetch it.

We never saw Mrs Drummond's daughters again. A man came to clear the house and it was put up for sale.

The day before I was due to go home again, we were sitting in the kitchen having breakfast, when we heard a soft knocking at the door. When we opened it, there was no-one there. Looking down, we saw a large parcel, done up in brown paper, lying on the step. We took it indoors and unwrapped it.

It was a patchwork quilt, one we had never seen before. A brilliant, shining thing made, not from cotton, but from silks and satins and velvet. Made from the rich dresses of three fat, expensive daughters. We stared at it in amazement.

"Well, Kate," Aunt Sarah said at last, smoothing it lovingly with her work-rough fingers. "Here's a beautiful thing."

"Now we have a quilt each," I said. "I like mine best."

"And I like mine," Aunt Sarah said. "Every time I see it, I'll be laughing. And there's nothing like a good laugh to keep you young."

## 3 The Strange Companions

I saw them first on the sea front at Brighton. There were few people about, for it was a grey afternoon, with a slicing wind coming off the sea. The two men were standing facing one another and seemed to be arguing, waving their arms about and clenching their fists. Two men, with their hair blowing sideways in dark streamers. Two men, each with the same long face, thin-nosed and frowning, each wearing a brown tweed coat and dark trousers. Even their shoes were alike; two-coloured, brown and white.

I had seen identical twins before, but only little ones, being wheeled along in those double push chairs. These were the first I had seen who were grown-up, and I remember being surprised that they should still choose to dress alike. They did not look the cheerful, joky sort of men who would enjoy confusing their friends. Their faces were full of misery, as if they found the world a bitter place.

I slowed down as I drew level, trying to see if I could spot any difference between them. I didn't think they would notice: they seemed so intent upon each other. But suddenly they both turned towards me.

One of them said, "What's the date, lad?"

"The date?" I repeated, surprised by the urgency in his voice. "Why, it's the third."

"The third? The third of what?"

"March."

"And the year?"

How could anyone forget the year? The day and the month, perhaps, if they were absent-minded, but the *year*! Was he having me on? I glanced at his twin, but he too was looking at me with the same anxious expression. Not even half a smile between the two of them.

"It's 1983," I said slowly.

"The third of March, 1983," he said, turning back to his twin. There was a kind of dismayed triumph in his voice, like someone who has won his point, only to find himself skewered on it. I was about to walk on and leave them to it, the twin idiots who didn't even know what year they were in, when they turned to me again.

"One more favour, lad," said the one who had spoken before. "Have you the time on you?"

"There's a clock over there," I said pointing.

"Yes. Ten to four it says. But is it *right*?"

I've been brought up to be polite, so I looked at my watch and nodded.

"It's ten to four, on the third of March, 1983," I said patiently. Not even sniggering.

"Seven years! Seven long years and five minutes *over*!" He glared at his twin and his twin glared back. On the long, sallow faces was the same look of bewildered despair. "Why aren't you gone? You should be gone! It's not fair! I've waited for this day, this hour, this minute ... Seven years I've waited. And five minutes over! Why are you still here? Go away, damn you! Leave me alone!"

I glanced quickly from one to the other, and saw on their faces an expression of tired hate.

It was obviously a family quarrel. A private quarrel. I could hardly stand there gawping, with my cold red ears sticking out. As I said, I've been well brought up. So I walked away, meaning to glance back later, to see if they had started to fight.

Before I had gone far, I heard footsteps running behind me and, turning, saw to my surprise that one of them – don't ask me which – had caught me up.

"I think I shall go mad!" he said.

Wrong tense. He already *was* mad, I thought. There was no future in it.

I said aloud, "What's the matter?" while my eyes searched the sea front for other people. It was deserted, but cars were passing on the road, and on the beach just below us, a woman was walking on the shingle with a small black dog.

"He should've gone," the man said. "It's not fair."

I looked back and saw his twin walking away from us along the cold, empty promenade.

"He is going," I said. "He's going now."

The man looked over his shoulder and at the same moment, his twin also turned. They glared at each other, and then both looked away.

We walked on in silence. It was getting darker now. Already the lights had come on, in bright skeins across the gloomy sky. I could hear the small dog barking and the waves crashing on the shingle.

"Here he comes," the man said.

I looked back again. I could just see the figure of his twin walking away into the twilight.

"No, he's still going," I said. "He'll soon be out of sight."

"Look in front of you," he said.

I looked. There was a figure coming towards us. A man, wearing a brown tweed coat and dark trousers. Even at this distance, I could see his shoes were two-coloured, brown and white. His dark hair was blowing sideways in the wind.

"But . . ." I looked back, bewildered, and there was the other one, still walking away in his brown tweed coat and dark trousers . . . "There're *three* of you!" I exclaimed. "Triplets!"

"No," said the man gloomily. "You don't understand."

I looked at him sideways and decided I didn't want to be alone with him any more, on the cold sea front, with the sky darkening, and only his replicas for company.

"Well – er – goodbye," I said. "I have to go now."

"Don't leave me, lad. Stay with me. I don't want to be alone."

"I'm sorry. I'm afraid I'm meeting someone. . ."

*"Please,"* he said, clutching my wrist with a thin, iron hand. "Please don't go. I need . . . I'd like to tell you my story."

"You're hurting me!" I said angrily, for one can carry good manners too far. "If you don't let go, I'll yell! There's a policeman across the road, in that doorway." (There might have been, for all one could tell from here.)

He let go of me immediately, apologising.

"Sorry, lad. I didn't mean to frighten you. Forgive me."

I nodded coldly and hurried towards the road. He came with me. I wasn't alarmed now, for there were cars passing only an arm's length away, and I could see people on the opposite pavement. I turned to him, intending to tell him to get lost. At the sight of his face, the words stuck on my lips. I had never seen anyone look so unhappy before.

"I might as well drown myself and be done with it," he said.

He stood, with his hands hanging limply by his side, and his face as cold and grey as the sky. Behind him, one of his brothers, if that's what they were, stood with his back to us, staring out to sea. I could no longer see the other.

"If they are bothering you," I said, "why don't you go to the police?"

He made a hopeless gesture and said nothing.

"Are they threatening you?" I asked, thinking of race gangs. There had been trouble in Brighton before.

He shook his head. "You don't understand," he said.

"Who are they? Are they your brothers?"

"No. There's . . . can I tell you about it? Will you let me come with you a little way? You won't be in any danger. I just want to tell someone."

Why me? Why not choose someone his own age?

"My father's a doctor," I said. "Perhaps he could help."

"He wouldn't believe me. He'd think I was mad." He looked at me and I tried to look back sympathetically, not as if I also thought he was mad. I was sorry for him. "I was once a lad like you," he said. "Just as clear-eyed and rosy-cheeked. Just as innocent. I envy you. Believe me, I envy you."

There was nothing much I could say to that. What did he know about me? I had my worries, too.

"I got into bad company," he said.

We had crossed the road now and were walking up Preston Street. People passed us, hunched into their coats, scarves fluttering like pennants. An old sheet of newspaper wrapped itself round my leg, then blew on, tumbling along the pavement in front of us. We turned into a side street to be out of the wind.

"I wasn't really wicked," he said. "Not wicked. You couldn't say I was wicked."

I was uneasy again. This narrow street was deserted. There were only two of us. I thought about turning back.

"I was just foolish. The usual things. Gambling, drink . . . It's so easy to drift into it. One always thinks one can turn back."

One can, I thought, and stopped, meaning to say I'd forgotten an errand for my mother in Preston Street. But then I noticed there was someone at the far end of the road, coming towards us. Relieved, I walked on.

"I lost my job, my money, my friends," the man said. "My real friends, I mean. I had plenty of companions, oh yes, all the riff-raff of the town made me welcome in their gutters. It's warm in the gutter and you'll find plenty of people to pull you down. Only it stinks, lad. It stinks like hell."

His face contorted – I almost thought he was going to cry. Embarrassed, I looked away from him, not wanting to be caught staring. The approaching figure was closer now. I could see it clearly. It was a man with dark dishevelled hair, wearing a brown tweed coat and dark trousers. His shoes were two-coloured, brown and white.

Startled, I turned and looked back. At the other end of the street a man was standing with his back to us. Dressed in a brown tweed coat, dark trousers and two-coloured shoes, brown and white.

"He won't hurt you," said my companion.

44

"Don't be afraid. Look, here's a café. Let's have some tea." He took hold of my arm and pulled me into a small, fly-blown café. I sat down at one of the formica-topped tables, while he went to get the tea. There were a young couple at the table opposite, and in the corner a big man who looked like a lorry driver, reassuringly strong. I looked out of the window into the street but could see no-one.

"Who are they?" I asked, as my companion came back to the table with the tea. "Who are those men?"

"I was telling you," he said, "I was just coming to it. Where had I got to?"

"You'd gone to the bad."

"Yes," he said, and sighed. He sat with his thin hands wrapped round his cup and the steam coming up round his chin; not drinking, just staring in front of him.

"What did you do exactly?" I asked curiously.

"Never you mind, lad!" he said sharply. "Things you're better off not knowing."

"But I thought you *wanted* to tell me . . ."

"Not that." He put down his cup, and straightened his shoulders. "Only what happened that day. The third of March. I'm sure it was the third," he said. "I was taking Clara out to lunch. We were engaged, we'd been engaged for years. She was a nice girl, good – not like the others. But just a little dull. Or so I thought then. Not that I wanted to break our engagement. I always meant to marry her in the end. Marry her and

45

settle down. We were to meet in the Palace restaurant at one o'clock. She was worried about me, the things I did. She wanted to save me from myself. I knew she'd be on at me to fix the wedding day. But I didn't want to get married yet . . . It was going to be difficult to explain. So I had a drink to give me courage. And another drink. . ."

He paused, and sipped his tea.

"What happened? Did you forget to go?"

"No, I went all right. I rolled into the restaurant, half an hour late, carrying a bunch of red roses which I dropped into someone's soup! It was tomato soup, I remember, and it splashed all over the cloth like blood."

"Did you do it on purpose?"

"No, of course not! There were all these little tables. Too close together. Lots and lots of little tables, and you had to weave in and out . . . I was drunk, of course."

"What happened then?"

"Clara broke off our engagement. Threw the ring at me. Oh, I didn't care then. Plenty more fish in the sea, I told myself, back in my room, with a bottle in my hand. There was this big mirror on the wall. It had belonged to my grandmother, and her grandmother before her. When I was a little boy, she'd say: 'Always look in the mirror before you leave the room, Billy, to see if you're fit for company.' I lurched towards it and saw this drunken idiot tottering towards me on rubber legs, grinning foolishly and waving a

46

bottle. This was what I'd made of myself. That sot!"

He put his cup down sharply on to the saucer. I saw his hands were trembling. But he seemed sober now.

"So did you decide to give it up?" I asked.

"Not then. No, I was giggling-drunk. I did a little dance in front of my reflection, waving my bottle and saying, 'Come, my fine fellow! Are you fit for company? You're the only friend I have left now. Just you and me and our bottles.' And my reflection giggled and capered with me . . . Suddenly I didn't like its face – my face – any more. So I threw the bottle at it. And the mirror broke."

He stopped and stared at me, with a look of remembered fright on his face.

"Was your grandmother cross?" I asked.

"My grandmother? No, no! She'd been dead a long time. It was the mirror! The mirror broke. . . ."

"*Seven years!*" I exclaimed. "Seven years' bad luck!"

"Seven years and – " he glanced at his watch, "and twenty minutes over. Why is he still hanging about?" He glared at me as if it were my fault.

"Who?"

"My reflection."

There was a long pause, in which we looked at each other in silence. Then we both glanced at the window. Through the glass, a face – his face – peered in at us. But this time there was another face beside it. Mine.

"It's dark outside," I said. "It's only the glass reflecting."

"You saw him, didn't you? On the sea front? In the street?"

"I saw two men."

"That's him! The mirror broke, the glass fell away – but he was still there! My reflection! For seven years, wherever I look, he's there. In front of me, behind me, beside me. Wherever I look. You saw him, didn't you? You saw him!"

I was trembling between belief and disbelief.

"I saw someone," I said doubtfully. "Some men. . ."

He smiled sadly, "You think I'm mad, don't you? Well, never mind, lad, perhaps I am."

He paid for our tea and we left the café together. As we walked down the street, I saw the figure – his twin? his reflection? – coming towards us. They stopped and looked at each other, without speaking. Facing each other. And their dark hair blew forwards over their eyes, as if there were two winds blowing, one from either end of the street. They stared at each other wearily, and never saw me go.

The following week, there was a report in the local paper, of a man found drowned. A Mr William Smith from Kemp Town. William. Billy . . . I was sure it was my reflected man. Drowning his sorrows in the cold grey sea. Why hadn't I

48

stayed with him, brought him home – anything but left him alone with his dismal reflections! I wished I hadn't run away.

So I was delighted, when the next day I saw him walking towards me, still wearing his tweed coat and dark trousers and two-coloured shoes. He was glancing about him, as if he were looking for someone. I looked round too, carefully, but could see no other men in sight.

I ran up to him, smiling. "He's gone at last, then?" I said. "You must've got the date wrong. Or the time. Perhaps it was later than you thought."

He looked at me briefly, and then away again as if I was not what he wanted to see. I was glad he looked away: his eyes had frightened me. They were so dark and desolate, as if cold winds were blowing in his head. His skin was waxen and his thin nose jutted out more sharply than I had remembered. He looked terrible.

"What's the matter?" I asked. "Aren't you well?"

He opened his mouth and his lips moved, but no sound came out.

"You're ill," I said. "Do you feel faint? My father's a doctor. He'll be able to help . . . Come home with me. It's just round the corner."

He stood there, looking round, like a dog who's lost his master. Like an abandoned child.

I took his hand in mine . . . It was glass-cold. A glass hand, smooth and fragile. I felt if I squeezed it, it would splinter in my fingers. I stared at him. But he looked so lost and pitiful, that I couldn't be frightened of the poor creature, whatever he was.

"Who are you?" I asked, and my breath smoked in the cold air. His face vanished. Above his collar, there was now only a greyish blur, as if I had breathed on a mirror. Yet still I held his glass hand in mine.

"It's no good looking for him," I said gently. "I think he's dead."

There was a sound of thin glass breaking; and he was gone. All that was left of him was a sparkle of tiny splinters, on my hand and on the pavement at my feet.

# 4  Siren Song

1 August 1981
Dear Tape Recorder,

This is me. My name's Roger and I'm nine years old today. You're my birthday present.

> Happy birthday to me,
> Happy birthday to you,
> Happy birthday, dear both-of-us . . .

1 August 1982

R for Roger. R for Roger. This is Roger, mark ten, calling. I'm not going to bore you with a bite-by-bite account of my birthday tea, like last year. This time I'll only record the exciting moments in my life. Over and out.

1 August 1983

My name is Roger Kent. I am eleven years old. I want to get this down in case anything happens to me.

I hate this village. I wish we hadn't come to live here. There's something funny about it.

For one thing, there are no other children here. Except Billy Watson, and he's weird. He's a thin, white-faced boy who jumps when you speak to him. Mum says he's been ill, and I must be kind. I was. I asked him to come to my birthday tea today. He twitched like I'd stabbed him in the back, and his eyes scuttled about like beetles. Then he mumbled something and ran off.

The grown-ups are peculiar, too. They're old and baggy-eyed, as if they'd been crying all night. When they see me, they stop talking. They watch me. It's a bit scary.

At first I thought they didn't like me. But it's not that. They look as if they know something terrible's going to happen to me, and are sorry about it.

Mrs Mason's the worst. I hate the way she looks at me. Her eyes are . . . I dunno . . . sort of hungry. I don't mean she's a cannibal. It's more like. . . D'you know why gerbils sometimes eat their own babies? It's because they're afraid they're in danger, and think they'll be safer back inside.

That's just how Mrs Mason looks at me. As if she'd like to swallow me to keep me safe. But what from?

This morning, when she heard it was my birthday, she hugged me. I jerked away. I didn't mean to be rude. I honestly thought she was going to start nibbling my ear. That's the sort of state I'm in.

"Never go out at night," she said. (That's nothing. Mum's always telling me that nowadays. It's what came next.) "Never go out at night, *whatever sounds you hear!*"

Funny thing to say, wasn't it? "Whatever sounds you hear."

I've been thinking and thinking, but I can't imagine what she meant. If we lived by the sea, I'd think of smugglers. You know, like that poem – "Watch the wall, my darling, while the gentlemen go by."

Perhaps they're witches! I'm not being silly. There *are* witches nowadays. It was in the papers once. COVEN OF WITCHES EXPOSED, it said. They certainly were exposed! There was this photograph of men and women with nothing on. Not that you could see much, only their backs. They didn't look wild and exciting at all. Just stupid. And cold – you could almost see the goosepimples. Still, they were witches.

D'you think it's that?

Full moon tonight. I'm going to stay awake and listen. It must be happening somewhere near enough for me to hear, or she wouldn't have said that.

Supposing they use our garden?

Suppose Mum's joined them! She's been a bit strange lately. No, that's silly.

10.30 p.m. I'm sitting by the window. Nothing's happened yet. Just the usual night noises, and not many of those. This village dies after ten o'clock. A dog barking. An owl getting on my nerves, can't the stupid thing say anything else?

It's boring. I think I'll go to bed for a bit.

0.00. I've got a digital clock and that's what it says. Like Time's laid eggs in a row. No time. Nothing point nothing nothing time. Don't count your minutes before they're hatched.

What's that?

Only an owl. The window's wide open, and it's cold. The moon is round and bright. There are shadows all over the garden. I can't see anything. It's very quiet now. No wind.

Listen!

*Children*! I can hear children laughing. I can hear their voices calling softly . . .

I think they're in Billy Watson's garden. He must be having a midnight party, and he hasn't asked me! Pig! No wonder he ran off when I invited him to tea.

I wish I could see them. There're too many trees. Too many shadows.

Listen!

This microphone's too small. I held it out of the window, but I didn't get anything.

They were singing. Their voices were high and clear. I could hear every word. It was a funny little tune. Sort of sad, but nice. There's a chorus where they all hoot softly like baby owls. I think I can remember the words –

"Little ghost, all dressed in white,
Walking on a summer's night,
(Hoooo, hooo,)
Calling to her childhood friend,
Asking him to come and play,
But his hair stands up on end.
Billy Watson runs away."

*Billy Watson*! So they are friends of his! I suppose they're playing a game . . .

Listen . . .

It was a girl singing alone this time. I'm sure it was a girl. Her voice was so high and sweet and sad, it made me ache. This is what she sang –

"Don't you love me any more?
I'm as pretty as before.
(Hooo, hooo,)
Though my roses all are gone,
Lily-white is just as sweet.
Stars shine through me now, not on
Flesh that's only so much meat."

I wish I could see her . . .

"Coo-ee! Over here!"

They heard me. I know they did. They're whispering. Now they're coming nearer. I can hear the bushes rustling by our wall. Look! I think one of them's slipped over into our garden. It's difficult to be sure. There are so many shadows. I'm going to dangle the microphone out of the window . . .

Listen!

> "Billy, see the moon is bright.
> Won't you play with me tonight?
> (Hooo, hooo,)
> Billy Watson's now in bed,
> With his fingers in his ears,
> And his blankets hide his head,
> And his face is wet with tears."

I got it that time! It's very faint, but you can just make out the words. I don't think they can be friends of Billy's after all. They sounded as if they were mocking him. I wonder who they are?

Oh, they're going away now! I can hear them running through the bushes. Laughing. They've gone!

No. There's still one standing in the shadow of the lilac tree. Just below my window. I'm sure it's the girl. I can see her white frock gleaming ... unless it's just moonlight. She's all alone now. Waiting for me.
Listen!

> "Little ghost all dressed in white
> Singing sadly in the night,
> (Hooo, hooo,)
> Who will play with me instead?
> Must I be lonely till the end?
> Is there any child abed
> Brave enough to be my friend?"

I'm coming! Wait for me! I know I promised Mum I'd never go out at night, but ... The moon is shining bright as day. Someone is singing in the garden below. Softly. Sweetly. Surely it won't matter if I go out just once?

The rest of the tape is blank. Roger Kent was never seen again.

# 5  A Change of Aunts

Everyone knows the pond in Teppit's Wood is haunted. A young nursemaid once drowned herself there. She had done it early one evening, with the sun sinking in the red sky, and the smoke from the burning house drifting through the trees.

They say she had slipped out to meet her sweetheart, and left the two little children alone, with the fire blazing behind its guard in the nursery grate. Burnt to cinders they were, the poor little ones, and the young nursemaid, mad with the guilt and grief of it, had done away with herself.

But she still can't rest, the tale goes; and at sunset, you'll see the smoke drifting through the trees, though a hundred years have passed since the big house burned down. Then, if you're wise, you'll run! For that's when the poor crazed ghost rises up, all wet from the dark pond, and goes seeking for the dead children. Searching and searching all through the woods for the little children . . . *Take care she doesn't get you*!

\* \* \*

Meg Thompson, who was eleven, thought perhaps she was too old to believe in ghosts. Her brother William believed in them, but he was only eight. Aunt Janet seemed to, but perhaps she was only pretending, just to keep William company, so that he need not feel ashamed.

Even in full daylight, Aunt Janet would hold their hands and run them past the pond, chanting the magic charm:

> "Lady of the little lake,
> Come not nigh, for pity's sake!
> Remember, when the sun is high,
> We may safely pass you by."

And they would race up the hill through the trees, until they arrived home, laughing, breathless and safe.

They loved Aunt Janet, who had looked after them ever since their mother had died. Unfortunately, a neighbour's brother, come visiting from Australia, loved her too, and carried her back to Adelaide as his bride.

That was when Aunt Gertrude came. She was as different from Aunt Janet as a hawk from a dove. Thin and hard and sharp, she seemed to wear her bones outside her skin and her eyes on stalks. She could see dirty fingernails through pockets, smuggled bedtime cats through blankets, and broken mugs through two layers of newspaper and a dustbin lid.

"I'm up to all your tricks," she told them, with a smile like stretched elastic.

She only smiled when their father was in the room. There were many things she only did when he was there, such as calling them her dears, and giving them biscuits for their tea, and letting them watch television. Just as there were many things she only did when their father was out, such as feeding them on stale bread and marge, slapping and punching them, and locking them in the cellar as punishment.

They did not mind being shut in the cellar. They played soldiers with the bottles of wine, or cricket with a lump of coal and a piece of wood. Or they sat on empty crates and planned vengeance on Aunt Gertrude.

"I'll get a gun and shoot her," William said. "I'll cut her up into little pieces with the carving knife and feed her to Tiddles."

"You'd only get sent to prison," Meg objected. "I'm going to write a letter to the Child Welfare and tell them about her, and they'll put *her* in prison."

"They won't believe you," William said, "any more than Dad does."

Meg was silent.

"Why doesn't Dad believe us?" William asked.

"Because she's always nicer to us when he's here. Because she doesn't hit us hard enough to leave bruises. Because she's told him we're liars." Meg hesitated, and then added slowly, "And because he doesn't *want* to believe us."

"Why not?"

"She's our last aunt. If she went, he wouldn't

know what to do with us. He might have to send us away, and that would be worse."

William looked doubtful, but before he could say anything, there was the sound of a door shutting upstairs.

"She's back! Look sad, William," Meg whispered. They did not want Aunt Gertrude to find out they did not mind being locked in the cellar. She'd only think of another punishment. One that hurt.

"Meg," William whispered anxiously, "you haven't told her about the haunted pond, have you?"

Meg shook her head.

"She'd take me down there, I know she would. At sunset," William whispered, his eyes huge with fear. "At sunset, when it's dangerous to go."

"I won't let her," Meg said.

In September, their father had to go to Germany for a month on business. They both cried when he left, and this made Aunt Gertrude angry. As a punishment, she sent them to bed without supper, locking their rooms so that they could not sneak down in the night to steal food from the kitchen.

"I'm up to all your little tricks," she told them.

They were so hungry the next day that they were almost glad it was Wednesday. For every Wednesday, Aunt Gertrude took them to tea with a friend of hers, who lived in Eggleston Street, three miles away by road and no buses. Mrs Brown was as square as Aunt Gertrude was angular, but otherwise seemed to be made of the same material. Granite. But at least they got sandwiches and cake there, and could shut their ears to the insults the two women aimed at them.

"The trouble I've had with them," Aunt Gertrude started off.

"I don't know what children are coming to, I'm sure," Mrs Brown agreed. And they went on and on until at last it was time to go.

The walk back was all up hill. Usually Aunt Gertrude would stride ahead, and shout at the children when they lagged behind. They never complained when their legs ached and blisters burst on their heels. They did not want Aunt Gertrude to find out about the short cut through Teppit's Wood. But this Wednesday, as they were getting ready to go, Aunt Gertrude said that she was tired.

"Looking after these two wears me out. I must tell John he'll have to buy me a car. It's a long walk back up Eggleston Hill. . ."

"Up Eggleston Hill?" Mrs Brown repeated, surprised. "Don't you take the short cut through the wood?"

The children looked at each other in alarm.

"What short cut?" Aunt Gertrude demanded. "I didn't know there was a short cut. Nobody told me. . ." Her eyes looked round for someone to blame, and found the children: "Did you know about the short cut?" she asked angrily.

"Of course they knew. Everyone knows," Mrs Brown said. She looked at Meg and William and smiled nastily. "Don't tell me you're afraid to pass the haunted pond? I thought only babies were afraid of ghosts!" The sinking sun, shining through the window, flushed her face as if with wine. "Never mind," she said, her voice as falsely sweet as honey from a wasp, "I'm sure your dear Aunt Gertrude will cure you of such silly fancies."

William clutched hold of Meg's hand.

"I'm not going through the wood! I'm not! You can't make us! Not at sunset!"

Meg put her arms round him. She could hear Mrs Brown telling Aunt Gertrude about the ghost of the young nursemaid, and Aunt Gertrude laughing scornfully.

"So you're frightened of ghosts, are you?" she said to the children, after they had left the house. "You'd let your poor aunt walk two unnecessary miles because of some stupid old wives' tale. Your poor aunt who works so hard while you spend all day playing! I'll soon see about that."

She grabbed them each by a wrist with her hard fingers, and dragged them down the path into the woods. The trees closed round them in a dark, whispering crowd, seeming to murmur, "The sun is setting . . . keep away, keep away!"

William began to struggle and kick. Aunt Gertrude let go of Meg and hit William so hard that he was knocked right off the path. He fell into a deep drift of dead leaves, which rose up like brown butterflies and settled down on to him, as he lay whimpering.

Meg ran to comfort him, "You'll have a big bruise," she whispered softly. "You'll have a big bruise to show Dad when he comes back."

He smiled through his tears.

"What's that? What are you two planning?" Aunt Gertrude asked sharply. "Any more nonsense out of you, and there's plenty more where that came from. Well? Are you going to behave?"

She stood over them, tall and thin and hard as an iron lamp-post, with the setting sun seeming to glow redly in her hateful eyes.

"Meg," William whispered, his arms round her neck, "I think she's a witch. Don't you? Meg, d'you think she's a witch?"

"No," Meg whispered back, more decidedly than she felt. "Come on, we'd better do what she says. Don't be frightened. I'll look after you, William."

So they walked down into the sighing woods. Their aunt marched behind them, throwing a long shadow that struck at their feet. William held tight to Meg's hand, and as soon as the dark pond came into sight, they began to chant under their breaths the words of the magic charm.

"Lady of the little lake,
Come not nigh, for pity's sake!
Remember, when the sun is high . . ."

"What are you two whispering about?" Aunt Gertrude demanded.

"Nothing," they answered.

For it was no good, the magic charm. It only

64

worked in daylight, when the sun was up. Now the sun had fallen into the trees, and the sky was on fire.

"Look!" William whispered.

Between the trees, pale wisps of smoke came curling and creeping over the ground, like blind fingers searching . . .

"It's the smoke! Meg, it's the smoke!" William screamed.

Aunt Gertrude grabbed his shoulder and shook him.

"Stop that din! Making an exhibition of yourself! It's only mist rising from the water. Come, I'll show you." She started dragging William towards the pond. Meg grabbed him by the other arm, and for a moment they pulled him between them, like a cracker. Then Aunt Gertrude hit Meg hard on the ear, and Meg let go, putting her hands to her ringing head.

Aunt Gertrude forced William to the very edge of the dark pond.

"There! Look down, there's nothing there, is there, you stupid little coward? Answer me! There's nothing there, is there?"

She was looking at William as she spoke. She did not see what both the children saw. She did not see what rose out of the pond behind her.

It was something dark and wet, a figure of water and weeds. Green mud clung like flesh to its washed bones. A frog crouched like a pumping heart in its cage of ivory. Its crazed eyes, silver as the scales of fishes, glared down at Aunt

65

Gertrude as she hit the terrified boy. It reached out . . .

Aunt Gertrude screamed.

William pulled away from her and ran. Blind with fear, he raced past Meg without seeing her, and disappeared into the trees.

Meg could not move. She crouched down on the damp, leafy ground and watched in terror. Dark water was torn from the pond in creamy tatters as the two figures struggled together, the screaming aunt and the other one, all water and weed and bone. Its silver eyes glinted, it fastened its ivory fingers like combs into Aunt Gertrude's hair. Down, down they sank in a boil of bubbles.

"Meg! Meg!" William's voice called from among the trees, and Meg, as if released, leaped to her feet and ran after him, leaving Aunt Gertrude in the pond.

William had fallen over. His knee was bleeding, his bruised face wet.

"Come on, come on, hurry!" Meg said, catching hold of his hand and dragging him after her.

For there was someone following. Running through the trees behind them, twigs snapping, leaves crunching under invisible feet.

"Run, William, faster, faster!" Meg cried.

"I can't!"

"You must! Run, William, run!"

It was nearer now, and nearer, following fast, bounding in huge leaps over the rotting branches and white nests of toadstools.

"Faster!" Meg cried, looking fearfully over her

shoulder at the shaking bushes, not seeing the twisted root that caught at her feet. She fell, bringing William down with her.

Aunt Gertrude burst through the bushes.

How strange she looked! She had run so fast that the clothes had dried on her body, and her cheeks were pink. Her hair, loosened from its tight knot, was tumbled and tangled about her head.

The children cowered away from her as she came up and knelt down beside them.

"Are you all right, my little dears?" she asked softly. (*Dears*?) "That was a nasty tumble! Why, you're shivering, Miss Margaret! And Master William, you've cut your poor knee." (*Miss*? *Master*?) "If you're a brave boy and don't cry, I'll give you a piggy-back home, and there'll be hot chocolate and cherry cake by the nursery fire."

They stared at her, trembling. The look in Aunt Gertrude's eyes was soft and kind. The smile on Aunt Gertrude's mouth was wide and sweet. What was she up to? What cruel trick was she playing now?

They were silent as Aunt Gertrude carried William up the hill to their home. There, as good as her word, she gave them hot chocolate and cake, and sat them on the sofa while she bathed William's knee.

When she had finished, she stood up and gazed at the empty grate in the living room, while they watched her silently. Then she left the room. They sipped their hot chocolate, sitting side by

67

side, listening. They could hear her going from room to room all over the house, as if looking for something.

"What's she up to?" William whispered.

"I don't know."

"Did you see it? Did you see it . . . in the pond?"

"Yes."

"What happened, Meg?"

"Aunt Gertrude fell in," Meg said, and shivered.

"Why is she so . . . so different?"

"I don't know."

"I wish Daddy were back," William said, and his lip quivered. Meg put her arm round him, and they were silent again, listening to the footsteps going round and round the house, slowly, uncertainly, as if Aunt Gertrude had lost her way.

There was no doubt that Aunt Gertrude was a changed woman since she had fallen into the pond. Perhaps the water had washed the nastiness out of her. The house had never been so bright and cheerful. Their meals had never been so delicious. She made them apple pie and cherry cake, and let them lick out the bowls. She played leap frog with them in the garden, and never minded running after the balls at cricket. She told them bedtime stories and kissed them good night.

William started calling her Aunt Trudie, and would often hold her hand, taking her to see some treasure; a large snail with a whirligig shell, a stone with a hole right through the middle or a jay's feather. Meg followed them silently, watching and listening. Once, when William did not know she was behind them, she heard him say:

"Aunt Trudie, you mustn't call us Miss Margaret and Master William, you know."

"Should I not, Master William?"

"No. Just plain Meg and William."

"William, then."

"That's better. And when Daddy comes home on Saturday, you must call him John. Can you remember that?"

She smiled and nodded.

"Don't worry," he said. "I'll look after you, Aunt Trudie." Then he caught sight of Meg behind them, and said quickly, "We're just playing a game. Go away, Meg! We don't want you!"

"Now, Mas . . . Now, William, that's no way to speak to your sister," Aunt Trudie said gently. "Of course, we want her." She smiled at Meg. "We are going to see the kittens next door. Come with us, Meg."

Meg shook her head and walked back to the house. She went up to Aunt Gertrude's bedroom and looked round. It was bright and clean, and there were flowers on the dressing-table. There was no smell, no sense of Aunt Gertrude in it anywhere. It seemed like another person's room. Meg sat down on the bed, and thought for a long time.

Aunt Trudie found her there, when she came in from the garden, flushed and laughing. She hesitated when she caught sight of Meg, then called over her shoulder, "Just a moment, William! Wait for me in the garden."

Then she shut the door and leaned against it, looking gravely and kindly at Meg.

"Will you be staying with us long?" Meg asked politely.

"As long as you want me to," was the answer.

There was a short silence. Then Meg jumped to her feet and put her arms round the woman.

"We don't want you to go, Aunt Trudie," she said. "We want you to stay with us for ever."

It was three years before Meg ventured once more into Teppit's Wood. She went in broad daylight, when the sun was high. It was curiosity that took her there, down the winding path to the dark pond at the bottom. It was a warm day and birds were singing in the trees. The pond looked peaceful. There was frogspawn in the brown water, leaves floated on the surface like little islands, and a water-boatman sculled across, leaving a silver wake behind him.

Meg stood a safe distance away and waited.

Bubbles began to disturb the quiet water. Now a scum of mud and filth rose slowly up from the bottom of the pond. It spread round a clump of frog-spawn, which shook and seemed to separate, and then reform into the shape of a hideous scowling face.

As she watched, Meg thought she heard, faintly, a familiar voice.

"Meg! Get me out! Get me out this minute! She's stolen my body, that wretched servant-girl! Meg, if you bring her down here, I'll give you a penny. I'll give you chocolate biscuits every day. And roast beef! Just bring her down here and push her in! Meg, I'll never hit you again, I promise, I promise, promise . . ."

"Goodbye, Aunt Gertrude," Meg said firmly, and left. That was the last time she ever walked in the woods round Teppit's pond.

# 6 The Good-Looking Boy

"Don't take any short cuts after dark," Anthony's mother was always telling him. "Come back by the main roads. Telephone if you're going to be late and I'll come and meet you."

She worried about him far more than she worried about his sister. This may have been because Nellie was three years older than he was, and clever enough to take care of herself. Or it may have been because Nellie was plain and fat, whereas he was so beautiful that his mother believed everyone who saw him must want to steal him away.

Anthony could not help knowing he was good-looking. Ever since his pram days, compliments had fluttered round his ears like butterflies – oh, what a lovely baby, what a handsome little fellow, what a pretty darling! Once, when he was four, a huge lady swooped at him crying, "Oh, you sweetie, I could eat you up!" And he had screamed and clung to his mother, seeing the large lip-sticked mouth coming at him, red as blood. His mother had laughed at him and told him it was only a saying people used, without meaning it. But for a long time after, he had had nightmares, waking up screaming in the dark.

Now he was ten, no-one called him pretty any more. They called him good-looking instead. All the girls at his school giggled and showed off in front of him. They invited him to their birthday parties, chose him for a dancing partner, and kissed him under the mistletoe at Christmas. Often the school wall would be decorated with hearts, drawn in chalk and inscribed: "Stella loves Tony" or "Claire loves Tony" and once, unkindly, "Tony loves Tony."

But he *wasn't* conceited! He knew he was not clever, like Nellie. Nor good at games, like his cousin John. He had no particular talents. It was just that, whenever his mother warned him not to walk through Queen's Wood after dark, or to accept lifts from strangers, he couldn't help seeing himself as a sort of delicious candy that everyone wanted to gobble up.

So he was a little nervous, when he disobeyed his mother one evening, and took the short cut through Bird Walk. The tennis courts on either side were deserted, for it was November and already dark at five o'clock. The lamps were screened by overhanging branches, whose bare twigs made a jigsaw on the concrete path, as if the world were coming apart.

He saw his shadow stretch and shrink as he walked. It seemed to be trying to get away from him, as if it knew something terrible was going to happen and didn't want to be involved. He wished now he had taken the long away home.

For there were footsteps behind him, ringing out sharply in the cold air. Hurrying when he hurried, running when he ran, clattering after him as he raced towards safety.

But the street was empty when he reached it: everyone was at tea. He fled down the pavement, and the footsteps came drumming after him, louder than his heart. They followed him home and down the path to the kitchen door. He dared not look round, dreading what he might see.

Coming at last into the warm, bright kitchen, he slammed the door shut behind him.

"Mum!" he called. "Mum, where are you?"

And heard the kitchen door slam again, as if the – the creature had followed him in. Trembling he turned round. There was no-one there.

"Hullo, darling, you're late," his mother said, coming in from the hall. "Why, what's happened?"

"Nothing," he said. He did not want to own up that he had taken a short cut home. That night he dreamed of vampires, and woke up screaming.

That was the first time he heard the footsteps. After that, he heard them always. Everywhere. In the school corridors, or walking the long way home with his friends, they were behind him, slowing when he slowed, hurrying when he hurried. Above the noise of the traffic and the chatter, he could hear them at his heels.

"What d'you keep looking round for?" his friends asked him.

"Nothing," he said.

For no-one seemed to be paying him any particular attention. No sinister figure dodged into a doorway. No foul face leered out of the shadows. Yet still the footsteps followed.

Then one evening, Tom Harlow, his best friend, said, "What a row your shoes make. You sound like a blinking carthorse. You've even got an echo."

"*An echo!*"

"Can't you hear it? Listen. Now stop. Now walk on again. See?"

"An echo!" Anthony cried, and shrieked with laughter and relief. It was only his shoes! The horrible heavy shoes his mother insisted he wore in winter. He'd been running away from his own feet!

It should be all right now that he knew what it was, but somehow the echo got on his nerves. He could not rid himself of the feeling that someone – something – was following him. He started wearing his plimsolls again, hiding his winter shoes in the garden shed on his way out, so that his mother would not know.

And still the footsteps followed him, squeaking softly on wet pavements or rustling in dry leaves. Stopping when he stopped. Running when he ran. Yet when he looked round, there was never anyone there.

Perhaps it's my ears, he thought. Perhaps I

wash them too often and I've worn away a sort of filter.

He stopped washing his ears. But still, through the dirt and wax, he heard the footsteps hurrying after him. Even in his own home, they followed him. Into the sitting-room, into the bathroom, into his bedroom, they came, whispering over the thick carpets. He began to wonder if he was going mad.

Then one day at school, his art teacher looked over his shoulder and said, "What's that you're drawing, Anthony?"

"A horse."

" – horse . . . horse . . ." The echo came so quick that it sounded as if he himself had repeated the word. He stared at Mr Watson in horror, but the teacher had noticed nothing amiss – except with Anthony's drawing.

"No, not like that," he said, correcting a few lines and adding a fourth leg. "There, that's better, isn't it?"

"Yes, sir."

" – sir . . . sir . . ."

This time Mr Watson did look at him curiously, but only raised an eyebrow and walked on.

After that, Anthony was afraid to open his mouth. But it was impossible to get through the school day without talking. The next lesson was English. His teacher wrote on the blackboard: "The daffodils dance merrily in the March winds."

"Now, Anthony, can you tell me which is the verb?"

Anthony was silent.

"Come on, we did verbs only yesterday. Well – "

"Dance, sir."

" – answer . . . answer . . ."

The other children laughed and Mr Field looked sharply at Anthony. However, seeing his pale face and nervous eyes, he said kindly, thinking the boy had stammered: "All right. Sit down. Now, you next, James. . ."

"What was all that dancer, answer business?" Tom asked, as he and Anthony were walking home.

"Nothing."

" – thing. . . thing . . ."

Tom laughed, thinking it was a gag. "Don't call me a thing, you clot, lot, lot," he said.

It was the start of a new craze. All Anthony's friends began repeating the last syllable. "You stink, ink, ink!" they shouted. "I want some chips, hips, hips!" and "Who's got my shoes, ooze, ooze?"

Among so many echoes, Anthony felt safe. Unnoticeable. But of course it could not last. People soon grew sick of it. Their parents shouted at them. Their teachers shouted at them.

"That's enough!" Mr Field roared. "The next child I hear doing that silly repetition had better look out! I won't warn you again."

The classroom was quiet. Mr Field's rages were respected.

"That's better," he said. "Now, where had we got to? Oh yes, William Blake. Very suitable. Seeing you're all so interested in repetition, note how he uses it. Page five, please. 'Tyger, tyger . . .' Anthony, will you read it for us, please."

It was an order. Not a question. Anthony stared at him helplessly. Why pick on him?

"Come on, boy. What's the matter? Have you found the page?"

Anthony nodded, and swallowed nervously.

"Hurry up, then. We're waiting."

If he had been clever, he might have thought of a way out. Fainted. Had a fit. Burst into tears. But his mind was blank with fright. Impelled by Mr Field's hypnotic eye and the expectant hush, he recited:

"Tyger, tyger, burning bright. . . ."

" – right . . . right . . ."

He was sent home.

That night he turned and tossed on his bed. His head ached. His thoughts revolved in his skull like clothes in a tumble dryer, all hot and tangled. What was he going to do? He daren't tell anyone . . . They'd think he was mad. Perhaps he was mad. What was he going to do?

The next morning, when his mother came to wake him, his face was flushed and his throat was so sore he could hardly speak. She took his temperature, and told him to stay in bed.

"You've got a cold," she said. He nodded happily and coughed. And there was nothing the echo could do but cough too, making him sound worse than he was. He wished he could have a cold for ever.

By the third day, when he had done the jigsaws and eaten all the grapes, he was a little bored. He opened one of the books his father had given him. Greek Myths. . . He yawned. They'd been to Greece for their holiday that summer. Super beaches. Too many old temples and statues and things. He was about to shut the book, when the word "Echo" caught his eye. He began to read.

"Echo was a nymph, who could no longer use her voice except in foolish repetition of another's words, as a punishment for talking too much. She fell in love with Narcissus, a Thespian, who was so beautiful that from an early age, his path was strewn with rejected lovers . . ."

Hearts chalked on a school wall . . . Anthony looked uneasily into the mirror opposite his bed. His reflection gazed back at him, pale, wide-eyed and – beautiful. He looked down at the book, and read on:

"She followed him everywhere, but could never tell her love, unable to do more than repeat his words. One day, Narcissus came to a stream, polished silver by the golden sun. He kneeled down to drink, and seeing his own reflection in the water, fell in love with it . . .

The words blurred. Anthony was back in Greece. A hot day. All morning he'd been dragged round to look at temples and statues. He'd been glad when it was time for their picnic. They sat down in the shade of some trees, by the side of a small silvered pool. Mum and Dad and Nellie had droned one and on about the things they had seen and read about. They were all so earnest. So clever. Except him! He had sighed wearily, and to comfort himself, smiled down at his reflection in the glassy water. . .

Had it started then? Had this horrible old nymph seen him? Confused him with Narcissus in her muddled mind and followed him home? Perhaps she had been dogging him ever since his holiday, and he hadn't noticed. Not until the night he'd taken a short cut in his new winter shoes.

"I'm not Narcissus!" he said to the empty room.

" – issus . . . issus . . ." Echo answered.

"I'm Anthony Glover."

" – lover. . . lover . . ." Echo said fondly.

He shivered, and looked once more at his book. There was no comfort there. In the end, Narcissus had stabbed himself, and been turned into the flower that bore his name. And Echo had mourned, "Alas . . . alas . . ."

He slammed the book shut. Looked again at the title. Myths? What were myths? They were just old stories, weren't they? Not like real history.

"It's not *true*!" he said aloud.

"Ooo!" Echo said disbelievingly. "Ooo!"

Lying in bed, with the sheet pulled up to his nose, he vowed he would never speak again.

After ten dumb days, Anthony was taken to the doctor, who shone a torch down his throat and into his ears and up his nose.

"There doesn't seem to be anything wrong," he said.

"But, doctor, he's lost his voice. He can't talk."

The doctor looked down at his notes for a long time. Then he looked up suddenly and said, "Well, what have you to say for yourself, young man?"

But Anthony was not so easily caught. He mouthed silently and pointed to his throat. The doctor shrugged and gave his mother a letter for the hospital.

At the hospital, he was examined by another doctor. A torch was shone down his throat and into his ears and up his nose. A flat piece of wood, like a lollipop stick, was pressed down on the back of his tongue, making him gag. A swab was taken from his throat.

The doctor looked puzzled. "Has he had some kind of shock?" he asked. "Trouble at school? Anything like that?"

Both Anthony and his mother shook their heads. After a moment, in which the doctor looked searchingly at Anthony, he gave them a prescription for a gargle and a tonic, and said it was nothing to worry about. Just a lazy throat. Come back in a month, if it's not better.

As they walked down the hospital corridor, Anthony could hear the footsteps trotting eagerly behind him, but his mother did not notice.

There was no question of his going back to school, for the Christmas holidays had begun. His uncle Bill rang up and offered them his cottage for a week.

"Just the thing," his father said when he heard of it. "All that fresh air will soon put Anthony to rights. Wrap him up warm, and he can't come to any harm. You'd like that, wouldn't you, Anthony? We can go to Echo Valley again. Remember how you loved shouting for the echoes when you were little?"

Anthony stared at him in horror.

"He was only small then," his mother said. "I don't suppose he remembers."

But Anthony did remember now. A little lake surrounded by hills. He, a small boy shouting, and the echo answering, answering, calling his name all round the sky.

"What's the matter, Anthony. Don't you feel well?"

He shook his head.

"It's been a tiring day. Better put him to bed."

Anthony lay awake for a long time, staring at the ceiling. Must he really be dumb for the rest of his life? No longer able to cheer his side at a football match. No longer able to run shrieking through the frosty streets. Unable to swap jokes with his friends. Already they were getting bored with one-sided conversations, and came to see him less often. Soon he would have no friends left at all. It wasn't fair! He hadn't asked to be born beautiful! He hadn't wanted Echo to love him! He wished she'd go away.

His eyes filled with tears. Perhaps the only thing to do was to stab himself, like poor old Narcissus. And turn into a stupid flower. Stuck in a vase for people to sniff at . . .

"No!" he shouted.

" – oh . . . oh . . ." Echo mourned.

His mother put her head round the door. "Did you call?" she asked hopefully. He shook his head and pointed to his throat, reminding her that he could not speak.

They arrived at Uncle Bill's cottage in the evening and, after supper, Anthony pretended he was tired and was sent to bed. For some time before he went to sleep, he lay listening to the sound of their voices in the room below. Talking, talking . . .

The next day was Sunday and everyone slept in late. Everyone except Anthony. He got up with the dawn, and dressed himself in his warmest clothes. Then he took something from his suitcase and put it in his pocket. He tiptoed silently down the stairs and let himself out of the house.

It was cold and he walked quickly, swinging his arms to keep warm. Above his head, pink clouds floated like sponges over the sky, washing the night away. A bird flew up from the bushes in front of him, singing in the rising sun. At last, he could see the little lake, held like a steel mirror in the palm of the hills. Echo Valley.

He ran down the hillside and came to the side of the lake. The water was cold and grey, scarcely ruffled by the wind. He crouched down beside it, shivering and fumbling in his pocket. Now he bent lower, towards his own reflection, and his hands went up to his face. One might have thought he was crying.

"Echo?" he called softly, not looking round.

"Echo! Echo!" she agreed.

"Are you coming?"

"Coming, coming!" she called gladly, and he thought he heard the grass rustle behind him.

He turned round. He was hideous! His face was bloated and spotted with green warts. His mouth was scarlet with blood. Two yellow tusks curved down to his chin.

"OH, YOU SWEETIE. I'M GOING TO EAT YOU UP!" he shouted.

Echo screamed. Aa-aah! The shrill sounds fled away to the hills. Fainter and fainter, they sounded. Then there was silence.

Anthony took off his rubber Dracula mask, and stood up.

"Echo?" he called softly.

Silence.

"Are you there?"

No answer.

"ARE YOU THERE?" he shouted.

But she never spoke to him again.

# 7  The Whisperer

The two girls walked silently down Appleford
Road. They did not link arms or laugh or even
look at one another. One of them looked miserable, almost frightened; the other was simply
cross. No-one would have taken them for best
friends.

The cross one was the first to speak. She was
a sturdy, freckled child, dressed with unaccus-
tomed neatness in a cotton frock and white socks.
Her hair was brushed and her fingernails clean.

"If it hurts that much to have me to tea,
Charlotte," she said, "let's forget it."

"Don't be silly, Jane," the miserable one said,
smiling with an effort. "If I hadn't wanted you to
come, I wouldn't have invited you."

"You didn't," Jane pointed out. "I had to ask
myself, remember?"

It still rankled. They had been best friends for
several months now, and Jane had had Charlotte
to tea hundreds of times. Never once had she
been asked back. Her mother had begun to
remark on it.

"Hullo, Charlotte, you here again?" she'd said;

and then to Jane when they were alone, "Hasn't that child got a home of her own to go to?"

"She lives in Appleford Road," Jane had said, hoping to silence her mother, for Appleford Road was very grand.

"Then you'd think they could afford to have you to tea for a change," her mother had retorted.

Jane was a careless, generous child; it hadn't occurred to her before to wonder why Charlotte had never invited her home. But now a small doubt, like a piece of grit in a shoe, began to prick her mind. Was Charlotte secretly ashamed of her? Was she just making use of her till she found some grander, more suitable girl to go round with?

"No! Charlotte isn't like that!" she had told herself. "There must be some other reason." Deciding to put it to the test, she had invited herself to tea.

So here she was at last, walking beside her unwilling friend (if friend was the word for her) going angrily to tea where she wasn't wanted and no longer wished to go.

"This is it," Charlotte said suddenly. She had stopped in front of a green-painted garden door in a high wall. Looking up, Jane could see the roof and chimneys of a house beyond it, showing dark against the sky. A hidden house. A shut-away, secretive house, quite unlike its ostentatious neighbours.

What have I got myself into? she wondered, suddenly uneasy.

To her surprise, Charlotte did not open the garden door, but instead rang a bell set in the wall beside it, and stood waiting.

"D'you always keep it locked?" Jane asked.

"Yes."

"Why?"

Charlotte shrugged and did not answer.

The door opened. Jane did not know what she had expected, but it was certainly not what she saw. A garden bright with flowers, a crowd of people, all laughing and talking and holding out their hands: welcoming her with every appearance of joy.

"Here's Charlotte's little friend at last!"

"We've heard so much about you."

"Come in, come in, my dear."

"We've been longing to meet you."

She was hugged and kissed and introduced all round. To her surprise, there turned out to be only four of them; Charlotte's mother and father and two uncles. Somehow they had managed to fill the garden with so much noise and gaiety, that Jane kept looking round to see if there was anyone she had missed.

It was the same when they sat down to tea. Huge mirrors on every wall reflected the loaded table. Silver teapots glittered wherever she looked, plates of cakes, dishes of crimson and emerald jellies multiplied themselves in endless reflections, and the laughing, chattering family became a multitude.

One, two, three, four of them, Jane counted

silently. And Charlotte and me makes six. The others are just in the mirrors. Why do I keep feeling there's someone else here? Perhaps there's a dog under the table.

She glanced down, but the long white table-cloth swept past her knees to the floor. She had no time to puzzle further, before she was drawn into the conversation. Her opinion was sought on this and that. Smiling questions were showered on her from all sides, so quick and so many she hardly had time to answer before the next one came. They flattered her, teased her gently, laughed uproariously when she ventured a joke.

I'm a success, she thought. They like me.

Glowing with pleasure, she looked across at Charlotte; and found her friend too was chattering and smiling. Jane had never known her so talkative before. Charlotte's eyes were brilliant and there was a feverish flush on her cheeks.

Feverish? Why had that word come into her head? Why wouldn't it go away again?

Suddenly, in spite of the sparkling room, Jane felt a growing uneasiness. She looked round the table and it seemed to her now that the people were as unreal as their reflections in the mirrors. There was something unnatural about them. Why did they all talk so much? Laugh so loudly? It was as if they were weaving a fence of sound to keep something out.

Again, and more strongly, she sensed there was someone else there. Someone she had not seen. She looked round, but there were no dark corners, no cupboards or hiding places. There was only the table, and its concealing cloth . . .

She let her napkin slide off her knees, as if by accident, and bent down to pick it up, hoping to lift the edge of the cloth at the same time. But one of the uncles bent down as quickly and their heads collided with a dull thud. In the instant of silence that followed this, Jane heard an urgent whisper, soft and plaintive, a child's voice.

"Please, please let me in . . .," it said.

Then they were all talking again, as loudly as ever, drowning out the small voice. Asking her if she was all right, apologising for the mishap, feeling her head for bumps, offering her more tea, and when she refused, suggesting she and Charlotte should go and play in the park . . .

"It's a lovely park, isn't it, Charlotte?"

"There's swings and seesaws."

"And ducks, don't forget the ducks!"

"And a grass bank to roll down. You'll love it there."

They had all got up together. Charlotte took her arm and pulled her towards the front door, while the others clustered behind her, still talking.

They want to get me out of the house, Jane thought, and, suddenly angry, she said loudly, "Can't I see your room first, Charlotte?"

Again, in the fleeting silence that followed her request, she heard the child's whisper.

"Let me in! Let . . ."

Then they were all talking again. Of course

she must see Charlotte's room. They would all go and see Charlotte's room. They would have a party there and play noisy games. Wouldn't that be fun? Then they'd all go to the park.

As they trooped upstairs, Jane managed to get next to Charlotte. She whispered fiercely in her ear, "Who's that child?"

But Charlotte did not seem to hear her. She was smiling and talking. Talking, talking. They were all talking together as if they would never stop. The sound of their voices pounded in Jane's head, until she longed to shout "SHUT UP!"

What would happen if she did? Would there be a shocked silence? Would she hear again the child whisper pleadingly, "Let me in. Please, let me in!"

She wished she had the courage to try it. Then a better idea occurred to her. One of the doors on the landing was half open, and on the wall she saw a roll of lavatory paper, its end swinging gently in the draught.

"Excuse me," she said, and before they could stop her, darted in, and shut and locked the door.

Silence. And then the whisper again, pleading, "Let me in! I promise I'll be good. Please let me in."

She looked round, puzzled, a little afraid.

"Where are you?" she asked. Outside the door, she could hear the muffled sound of voices, still talking as if they hoped to drown out the small voice. But the door was too thick.

"Let me in! Won't you let me in?" a child whispered.

Jane put down the seat and, kneeling on it, looked out of the window. The garden below was empty. There was no-one perched in the branches of the nearby trees. A small wind, like a sigh, blew through the open window, and she shivered.

Still the voice pleaded, "Let me in! Let me in!"

When Jane came out, Charlotte was waiting for her on the landing. She was alone. The false animation had left her face. She looked pale and tired.

"So now you know," she said.

Close by, a child whispered incessantly, "Let me in! Let me in!"

"Where is it?" Jane asked nervously.

Charlotte shrugged. "In the house. In the garden. Not outside the walls, thank heavens! It doesn't do anything. Just whispers. On and on and on till we could scream. We turn the radio up loud, or the telly – the whole house shakes with noise and our heads ache, and still we know it's there. Even in my sleep I hear it, knocking softly on my head, asking to be let in. I *hate* it!"

"Why don't you move house?" Jane asked.

"You don't understand," Charlotte said. "We didn't find it here. We brought it with us. It's ours."

"Let me in. Please let me in," the child whispered. "I want to play with you."

\* \* \*

They went to the park after all, running all the way there, racing away from the sound of a radio turned up too loud and a child's whisper. It was quiet in the park. There were not many people about. Most of the children had already gone home to supper. An old lady was throwing slices of bread from a wrapped loaf into the pond. The ducks pecked at it halfheartedly.

"They used to take her to feed the ducks," Charlotte said. "It wasn't as if they were horrid to her."

"Who?"

"My father's little sister. Mary. She'd have been my aunt if she'd lived. I don't know if you can be an aunt if you're already dead, do you?"

Nearby, some boys were kicking a ball about on the grass. They had put some sweaters down to mark a goal mouth, and they cheered as the ball went sailing through. As it bounced off the ground, a little girl ran forward to catch it, and missed. It slipped through her fingers and hit her cheek. She began to cry.

"It's yer own fault," an older boy said roughly. "Why didn't yer stay at 'ome like I told yer to?"

"I wanna play," the little girl whined. "I wanna play with yer, Mike."

"It must have been like that," Charlotte said, watching the little girl. "I wonder if her name is Mary, too. If so, those boys had better watch out."

"What happened?" Jane asked.

"Nothing much! That's what's so unfair," Charlotte said angrily. "She was too young, that's all. Dad was eight when she was born, and Uncle Peter and Uncle Mark even older. There'd just been the three of them before, you see."

"Didn't they want a baby sister?"

"I don't know. I don't suppose they minded," Charlotte said, shrugging. "Dad said they quite liked her when she was in her pram. Or tucked up in her cot with her teddy bear. It was when she could walk, that's when the trouble started. She was always tagging after them, wanting to play."

The little girl in the park was sitting on the ground now, sucking her thumb. Her eyes followed the ball longingly.

"Didn't they let her? I mean, not ever?" Jane asked.

"Yes! Sometimes. They weren't horrid to her. But – well Dad said Mary was so clumsy. She always fell down and hurt herself, and they'd be blamed. She couldn't climb trees. She couldn't play cricket. Three of her front teeth were knocked out once. Dad said she just stood there, watching the ball coming, and didn't even have the sense to duck. It was only her milk teeth, but they got into a terrible row."

"Did they begin to hate her then?" Jane asked.

"*No*! They never *hated* her! They just didn't want her around all the time. When they were in their room, they'd bolt the door. They'd hear her outside, wailing, 'Let me in! Please let me in!' and they'd shout at her to go away. You can't blame them. She always broke their things. She didn't mean to, and she'd be sorry and cry."

"Poor Mary," Jane said, remembering the forlorn whisper. "I expect she was lonely."

"Don't take her side!" Charlotte said sharply. "Suppose she was sorry? Tears don't mean anything, do they? How'd you like *her* hanging around you all the time?" She gestured towards the little girl in front of them. "Would you like her following us everywhere, butting in, breaking our things?"

The little girl was standing up again, scratching her leg and sniffing. Then she started running after the ball. A boy charged into her, knocking her over.

"Mike, 'e 'urt me! Mike!" she wailed, but her brother took no notice.

"She shouldn't have got in the way," Charlotte said, and Jane did not know which child she meant, the living or the dead.

"What happened in the end?" she asked.

"There was a terrible quarrel. My father had been making a model aeroplane, a big one. He'd spent weeks on it, and it was nearly finished. It was a beauty, he said. He was very proud of it. He couldn't lock his door. The key was lost. But he'd warned Mary that she must never, never go into his room when he was out, or something horrible would happen to her . . ."

"And she did?"

"Yes. He came back from school one day and found her sitting on the floor, crying, with all the broken pieces around her. 'I'm mending it for you, Johnny,' she said, looking frightened. 'I'm putting it together again.' He lost his temper. You can't blame him. Anyone would have done. He pushed her from the room, shouting at the top of his voice, 'Get out and stay out! Don't come near me again as long as you live! I hate you!'" Charlotte was silent for a moment, then she said stubbornly, "You can't blame him."

"No," Jane agreed.

"She was taken ill that night, and rushed to hospital. He never saw her again. They said she was too weak for visitors. And she died. She just seemed to fade away. It was nothing to do with him. But he thought it was his fault. It was then the whispering started."

It was still quite early when they came back from the park, only half-past six. The warm evening sunlight polished the green door till it shone like an emerald.

"Don't go yet," Charlotte begged. "Stay a bit longer."

Jane hesitated. The atmosphere of the hidden house, the over-loud voices and the frantic laughter remained in her mind like a bad taste. And the small voice whispering ... poor little girl, she thought, and shivered.

"People never want to come again," Charlotte said bitterly. "They're interested, they want to hear all about it, but suddenly they don't want to know us any more. It's as if we had the plague."

"I'm not scared," Jane said untruthfully. "I'll come in. I don't have to be back yet."

Charlotte's face brightened. She opened the door with a key, saying slyly, "No need to warn them now, since you've found out. Let's stay out in the garden and talk. I'll just tell them we're back." And she ran off into the house, leaving Jane alone.

Jane walked idly over the lawn, looking unseeingly at the flowers, her mind full of what she'd heard. She stepped on something that rolled beneath her foot, nearly unbalancing her. Looking down, she saw it was an old tennis ball, nearly as green as the grass. She picked it up and began tossing it into the air and catching it again . . .

"Let me in," the child whispered. "Please let me in."

Jane swung round, her heart racing. She had thought she was safe in the garden. Slowly she began backing towards the wall.

"Go away!" she said fiercely.

"Let me in," the child implored. "I'll be good. I promise I'll be good." It was such a piteous sound, the voice of a child who had been crying in the dark too long, that it touched Jane's heart. She could not send it away.

"I want to play with you," the child whispered. "Please let me play with you."

"Where are you?"

"Here."

"Catch!" Jane threw the tennis ball in the air.

It fell unchecked and bounced across the grass. I've gone mad, she thought, watching it. But then there was a sound of quick, excited breathing, and the voice said, "I'll get it! I'll get it!"

Jane saw the ball rise up from the ground and hang in the air like a stained moon. Then it came sailing towards her, a feeble throw that would have fallen short, had she not raced forwards and scooped it up, her knuckles grazing the grass.

"Where are you?" she asked again.

"Here."

She tossed the ball to where the voice had seemed to come from, and saw it stop suddenly, caught in invisible hands.

"Well done!" she cried, and heard the child laugh gleefully.

Jane was suddenly filled with wild excitement. All her fear was gone, replaced by a strange joy. "Throw it again!" she called. "Let's have a game!"

The ball flew towards her, a high, arching shot. Before she could jump for it, a hand reached over her head and caught it. Startled, she looked round.

Three tall men stood behind her, Charlotte's father and her two uncles. Behind them, Jane saw her friend, coming slowly over the grass, her eyes wide and nervous. It was Charlotte's father who had caught the ball. Jane noticed for the first time, now that he was no longer talking and laughing, how tired he looked. There were deep lines on his forehead and round his mouth.

"Hullo, Mary," he said softly, looking over Jane's head to the empty grass, as if he longed to see someone standing there. His face seemed to waver, as if it were a reflection in disturbed water. The lines of age became bars through which a boy's face looked out pleadingly.

"Can we play too?" he asked, almost timidly, and tossed the ball gently in the air. It came back so fast that he missed it, and the invisible child squealed with laughter, calling out, "Butterfingers! Who's butterfingers now?"

A strange game began on the sunlit lawn, three men and two girls running and leaping and shouting, playing with a ghost child they could hear, but could not see. Her cries rang out in the evening air, sweet as a bird.

"Here I am! Not there, silly! Missed again!"

And the three middle-aged men ran about like boys, shouting, "Over here! Jump for it! Oh, well done, Mary! Did you see that catch?"

At last, out of breath, they stopped. The ball fell to the grass and rolled slowly away.

The child said, "I've got to go now. Time for bed. You're not cross with me any more, are you, Johnny?"

Charlotte's father said gently, "No, Mary. I'm not cross, little sister. Go to your sleep."

The voice was further away when it spoke again. Very soft, very joyful.

"Good night," it said. "Good night, good night!"

Then there was silence. Nobody spoke. Jane and Charlotte and the three men stood still as

98

statues. Leaves shifted in the wind above their heads. A bird called from a tree. Some gardens away, someone was pushing a lawn-mower backwards and forwards. It was a beautiful summer evening, washed by a golden sun.

"I'd forgotten," Charlotte's father said, and though his voice was unsteady, he was smiling. "Poor little monkey-face, she never could go to sleep till we'd made it up. I'd forgotten that."

## 8   A Fall of Snow

Jake Benson was a winter boy. Born one white January, with the snow falling heavily outside, just as it was now, he had turned his red, crumpled face to the window, and smiled to see it. Or so his mother claimed.

Certainly he had always loved snow. Even now, as he sat looking miserably out of the classroom window, the sight of the tiny whirling flakes comforted him.

After all, he thought, it was Timothy's own fault. If he hadn't dawdled over his lunch, making patterns in his mashed potatoes with his fork, chasing each separate pea around his plate, we wouldn't have run into the bully-gang in the corridor. All the first form knew they were looking for a new victim. And there was Timothy, such an obvious choice, small and pale, his pink nose like a white rabbit's, twitching with terror.

What did he expect me to do? Jake thought. There were four of them, great third form louts, what could I have done? It'd just have made things worse . . .

He glanced towards Timothy. Timothy was

sitting hunched over his book, his chin in his hands, his fingers spread to hide the tear stains on his cheeks. He had not said a word since he had come back. Had avoided Jake's eyes ever since that last imploring look in the corridor after lunch, when the bully-gang had closed in on him.

"Hey, you! What's-yer-name, you with the fancy curls. We want a word with you!" they'd said, surrounding Timothy, herding him towards the door to the playground. And Jake had run away.

He did not see what else he could have done. They were both new boys, solitary boys, usually to be found on the edge of chattering groups, smiling uneasily. And because they sat next to each other in class, they had started going about together, waiting for one another so that they could travel on the same bus home.

But we're not friends exactly, Jake thought, I don't owe him anything.

Outside the window, the snow fell constantly, silently covering up the flawed concrete paths, the bedraggled winter hedges, covering up the stains of the day.

I'll make it up with him on the bus going home, Jake decided, I'll explain . . . what? That I'm a coward? That I was glad they'd picked on him and not on me? That I never even thought of telling one of the teachers . . .

Oh hell, I'll make up something, some excuse. I'll say I tried to find Mr Tinker, old Stinker on

101

playground duty, blind as a bat with the snow on his spectacles and no windscreen wipers. I'll think of something.

He did not have a chance. When the final bell went, Timothy snatched up his books and bolted. Jake, hurrying after him, was caught by Mr Becker with some silly query about his homework. When he got to the cloakroom, Timothy was not there.

"Timothy Sinclair? He's been gone ages," one of the boys told him. "Been crying, hadn't he?"

"Dunno," Jake mumbled, and hurried away.

On the bus going home, he sat looking sadly out of the window. The snow, tarnished by the sodium lighting, was all trampled on the pavements. It fell lightly now, separate flakes that could do no more than speckle the ugly scraped areas outside the shops, where the earlier snow had been shovelled away into dirty heaps in the gutters.

Why do they always spoil it? Jake thought.

He got off at Tatten's Corner, and started to walk home. And there on the Common, the snow lay in all its glory; deep and crisp and even, like a Christmas carol. Bushes gleamed like white coral in the liquid dusk. The frozen trees stood out against the soft radiance of the snowlight, the earth brighter than the sky. Not a mark, not a footprint marred its innocent perfection.

Jake stood and stared at it longingly. Never cross the Common by yourself, his mother had warned him, and Jake had promised, remembering the headlines in the local paper: woman found stabbed, old man mugged, child missing.

Tonight, he hesitated. All that untrodden snow, just waiting for him! Why shouldn't he, just this once? He had had such a horrible day. And it was safe. No murderer or mugger could be hiding behind a bush, waiting to spring out on him. There was no way they could have got there without marking the snow. Not unless they could fly!

He glanced round. There was no-one to see him.

Slowly Jake left the trampled pavement and the safety of the street lamps, and walked out on to the Common.

He was an Arctic explorer. He was a spaceman, setting foot on the frozen dust of some strange planet. He was a yeti, striding across the white wastes of the Himalayas. He was the king of Winter . . .

*Who's that!*

He was a small boy again, a frightened boy, swerving away from the figure that barred his way, trying to run and skidding . . . With a cry, he fell into a cold bed of snow and lay trembling.

He looked up. It was only a snowman! A huge snowman standing like a sentinel beside the path. Those were just black pebbles in its head, that seemed to stare at him so threateningly. It was only compacted snow, not a white stocking over its face. Its ugly slit of a mouth was merely a small twig.

Jake got slowly to his feet and walked up to it. What an ugly mug! There was something familiar about those clumsy, lumpish features, the mean eyes, the thick shoulders . . . *Art Waller!* That's who it reminded him of! Art Waller, the leader of the bully-gang. Art Waller who had made him desert his friend.

All the misery and shame of his day exploded into anger. He smashed his fist into the smirking white face, and saw with fierce joy the cold flesh crack. Half the head slid down over the huge shoulders and fell to the ground. Still the remaining eye was fixed on him, with an unblinking stare.

Plucking a half-buried stick out of the ground, he fell upon the figure, stabbing and slicing and smashing, kicking it with his feet.

"That's for Timothy!" he shouted. "And that's for me! And that's for all of us you turn into cowards and sneaks! Take that!"

When at last he stopped, flushed and panting, there was only a pile of battered snow at his feet. He turned away, feeling slightly sick, somehow ashamed. His boots crunched into the deep snow as he walked, but the pleasure had gone out of it. And he seemed to have strayed off the path; there were bushes in front of him, barring his way.

He turned, meaning to retrace his steps. Turned and stood staring. There were footprints in the snow behind him. Not his own. Huge footprints, monstrous footprints! And they were moving. They were coming after him.

He could see no-one. Nothing but footprints, biting heavily into the deep snow to the cold earth beneath. There were the prints of animals as well. He saw the rosettes made by their invisible paws, running from side to side, as if sniffing him out.

In terror, he turned and ran, slipping and skidding, crashing into the frozen bushes, dislodging little avalanches of snow. And every time he looked over his shoulder, he could see the footprints hurrying after him, faster and faster.

Now he came to a round clearing, a white circle like a huge spotlight. As he hesitated, wondering which way to go, he saw footprints coming out of the bushes in front of him; from every side they came, closing in on him.

With a cry of despair, he raced to the nearest tree. His gloved fingers scrabbling on the frozen bark, somehow he managed to pull himself up on to a branch. When he looked down, he saw the footprints had encircled the tree. Here and there, there was a soft flurry in the snow, as if some large, invisible animal had sat down to wait. The wind howled like wolves in the branches. And all the time, a terrible sense of evil steamed up from the ground below him. It was as if by his own violence, by smashing the snowman, he had let loose an answering violence in the night.

He could not hold on for long. Already he could no longer feel the branch beneath his fingers and his legs were becoming numb. Sooner or later he would slip and fall, and he knew when he did, it would be the end of him. He tried to call for help, but all that escaped his cold lips was his panting breath, sending up little smoke signals of distress into the freezing air. It seemed the most terrible thing of all that it was the snow that had betrayed him, the snow he had always loved.

The world tilted before his eyes. He felt his fingers slipping. Help me, he prayed.

And suddenly it began to snow again, tiny flakes, each no bigger than the head of a pin. Faster and faster they fell, in thousands and millions, tumbling from the dark sky. And the footprints began to move once more, running backwards and forwards as if trying to escape. The tiny flakes were smothering them, obliterating them; already they were no more than shallow indentations, scampering about in panic. Still the snow fell remorselessly, wiping them out.

There was nothing below Jake, as he tumbled out of the tree, but a smooth, immaculate whiteness. He lay there, stiff as an icicle, his hot tears freckling the snow beneath his cheek. The snow fell gently on him, covering him, hiding him. He had only to shut his eyes and lie, safe in this soft, cold bed, and nothing could ever hurt him again. But even as he thought this, a lump of snow, falling from the tree, slapped his face. He could hear the whisper of the flakes as they hit his anorak, trying to tell him something. Little fingers of ice poked him.

"What d'you want me to do?" he said aloud,

and sat up, brushing the snow from his clothes, beating his cold legs with his colder hands, until they came back to life.

All around him, the snow flakes whispered, in the trees, in the bushes, but he could not understand what they were saying.

When at last Jake staggered off the Common and down the pavement, he saw a boy standing under the lamp-post outside his house. It was Timothy, his hands in his pockets, the hood of his anorak pulled tightly around his small, pale, unsmiling face. Jake walked up and stood in front of him, not speaking.

"Why're you hobbling like that?" Timothy asked.

"Fell out of a tree."

"Daft."

"Yeah. Wanna come in with me?"

"Might as well."

They turned and walked together towards the lighted house.

"Sorry about – you know, after lunch," Jake said awkwardly.

Timothy shrugged: "Nothing you could do."

Was there really nothing? Jake wondered.

The snow fell on them as they walked, freckling their anoraks, forming white epaulettes on their shoulders. Jake held out his hand and saw the flakes fall, and melt, and fall again until his navy woollen glove was covered. Funny stuff snow, he thought, weak and wet and soft – and yet so powerful!

Suddenly he smiled. He knew at last what the snow was trying to tell him. There *was* something. In his mind he saw an avalanche of first form boys, falling upon the bully-gang. The whole of 1a and 1b and 1c, joining together to smother them, to wipe them out for ever.

# 9  QWERTYUIOP

Jobs don't grow on trees, the principal of Belmont Secretarial College was fond of saying.

"Be positive," Mrs Price told her departing students, as she shook them by the hand in turn. "Go out into the world and *win*! I have every confidence in you."

When she came to her last student, however, her confidence suddenly evaporated. She looked at Lucy Beck, and sighed.

"Good luck, my dear," she said kindly, but rather in the tone of voice of someone wishing a snowman a happy summer.

Lucy Beck was young and small and mouse-coloured, easily overlooked. She had a lonely "O" level and a typing speed that would make a tortoise laugh.

"Whoever will want to employ me?" she had asked Mrs Price once, and Mrs Price had been at a loss to answer.

Lucy wanted a job. More than anyone, more than anything, she wanted a job. She was tired of being poor. She was fed up with macaroni cheese and baked beans. She was sick of second-hand clothes.

"We are jumble sailors on the rough sea of life," her mother would say.

Lucy loved her mother, but could not help wishing she would sometimes lose her temper. Shout. Scream. Throw saucepans at the spinning, grinning head of Uncle Bert.

If I get a job, I'm getting out. He's not drinking up my pay packet, that's for sure. *If* I get a job ... Trouble was that there were hundreds after every vacancy, brighter than Lucy, better qualified than Lucy, wearing strings of "O" levels round their necks like pearls.

Who in their right minds will choose me? Lucy wondered, setting off for her first interview.

So she was astonished to be greeted by Mr Ross, of Ross and Bannister's, with enormous enthusiasm. She was smiled at, shaken by the hand, given tea and biscuits, and told that her single "O" level was the very one they had been looking for. Then she was offered the job.

"I hope you will be happy here," Mr Ross said, showing her out. There was a sudden doubt in his voice, a hint of anxiety behind his smile, but she was too excited to notice.

"I've got the job! I've got the job!" she cried, running into the kitchen at home. "I'm to start on Monday. I'm to be paid on Friday."

Her mother turned to stare at her.

"You never! Fancy that now! Who'd have thought it!" she said in astonishment.

Lucy was not offended by her mother's surprise. She shared it. They never trusted luck, but

110

looked at it suspiciously, as if at a stranger coming late to their door.

Ross and Bannister's was a small firm, with a factory just outside the town, making cushions and duvets; and an office in the High Street. On Monday morning, at ten to nine, the door to this office was shut and locked.

She was early. She smoothed down her windy hair, and waited.

At five-past nine, an elderly man, with small dark eyes like currants and a thick icing of white hair, came hobbling up the stairs. He was jingling a bunch of keys.

"Ah," he said, noticing Lucy. "Punctuality is the courtesy of kings, – but a hard necessity for new brooms, eh? You *are* the new broom, I suppose? Not an impatient customer waiting to see our new range of sunburst cushions, by any chance?"

"I'm Lucy Beck," she said, adding proudly, "the new secretary."

"Let's hope you stay longer than the other ones," the man said, and unlocked the door. "Come in, come in, Miss Beck. Come into the parlour, said the spider to the fly. I'm Harry Darke, thirty years with Ross and Bannister's, retired with a silver watch, and now come back to haunt the place. Can't keep away, you see." Then he added oddly, half under his breath, "Like someone else I could mention, but won't."

He looked at Lucy, standing shy and awkward, clutching her bag and uncertain what to do.

"Poor Miss Beck, you mustn't mind old Harry. Part-time messenger, office boy, tea-maker, mender of fuses. Anything you want, just ask old Harry. Mr Ross is down at the factory in the morning, but he's left you plenty of work to be getting on with." He pointed to a pile of tapes on the desk. "Letters to be typed, those are. He got behindhand, with the last girl leaving so quick. Left the same day she came. Shot off like a scalded cat!"

"Why?" Lucy asked curiously.

"Hang your coat in the cupboard here," he said, ignoring her question. "Washroom along the passage to the right. Kitchenette to the left. We share it with Lurke and Dare, House Agents, and Mark Tower, Solicitor. No gossiping over the teapots, mind. Most of the young things go to Tom's Café for lunch. Put this sign on the door when you leave." He handed her a cardboard notice on a looped string, on which was printed: Gone For Lunch. Back At Two. "Now is there anything else you want to know before I slope off?"

"You're going?" Lucy asked, surprised.

"Yes, my girl. I've errands to do. Not frightened of holding the fort on your own, are you?"

"No, but . . ."

"You can take a telephone message without getting the names muddled, can't you?"

"Yes, of course."

"Nothing else to it, is there? No need to look like a frightened mouse.

"I'm *not!*"

He looked at her for a long moment, with a strange expression on his face, almost as if he were sorry for her.

"You're very young," he said at last.

"I'm seventeen."

"Don't look it. Look as if you should be still at school. This your first job?"

"Yes."

He shook his head slowly, still regarding her with that odd pity.

"It's a shame," he said; then, seeing her puzzled face, added briskly, "Well, I'll be off then. Mr Ross will be in this afternoon."

Yet still he stood there, looking at her. Embarrassed, Lucy turned away and took the cover off the typewriter.

"Just one last thing," the old man said, "that's an electric typewriter."

"I'm used to electric typewriters," Lucy said coldly. She was beginning to be annoyed.

"Not this one. This one's . . . different. You mustn't worry," he said gently, "if it goes a little wrong now and again. Just ignore it. Don't bother to re-type the letters. Splash on the old correcting fluid. Look, I got you a big bottle. Liquid Paper, the things they invent! And if that runs out, cross out the mistakes with a black pen – see, I've put one in your tray. Nice and thick, it is. That should keep her quiet."

"I don't make mistakes," Lucy said; then honesty compelled her to add, "well, not very many. I've been trained. I've got a diploma."

"Yes. Yes, my dear, so they all had," he said sadly, and left.

After the first moments of strangeness, Lucy was glad to be alone. No-one breathing down her neck. She looked round the office with pleasure. Hers.

Sunlight streamed through the window. The curtains shifted a little in the spring breeze. There was a small blue and green rug on the floor.

I'll have daffodils in a blue vase, Lucy thought. I can afford flowers now. Or I will be able to, on Friday.

Better get on with the work. She sat down, switched on the typewriter, inserted paper and carbons, and started the first tape.

"Take a letter to Messrs. Black and Hawkins, 28, Market Street, Cardington. Dear Sirs . . ." Mr Ross's voice came clearly and slowly out of the tape deck. Lucy began to type.

She was a touch-typist. She did not need to look at the keys. Her fingers kept up their slow, steady rhythm, while her eyes dreamed round the office, out of the window, down into the sunny street.

". . . our new line of sunburst cushions in yellow, orange and pink," came Mr Ross's voice.

There was something odd! A sudden wrong-

114

ness felt by her fingers, a tingling, an icy pricking . . .

She snatched her fingers away and stared at the typewriter. It hummed back at her innocently. What was wrong? There was something . . . Her glance fell on the incompleted letter.

Dear Sirs,
    I am pleased to inform you that QWERTY-UIOP and Bannister's have introduced a new QWERTYUIOP of sunburst cushions in QWE-RTYUIOP, orange and QWERTYUIOP . . .

She stared at it in horrified bewilderment. What had happened? What had she done? Not even on her first day at the Belmont Secretarial College had she made such ridiculous mistakes. Such strange mistakes – QWERTYUIOP, the top line of letters on a typewriter, repeated over and over again! Thank God there had been no-one to notice. They'd think she had gone mad.

She must be more careful. Keep her mind on the job, not allow it to wander out of the window into the sunny shopping street below. Putting fresh paper into the typewriter, she began again.

She was tempted to look at the keyboard . . . "Don't look at the keys! Keep your eyes away!" Mrs Price was always saying. "No peeping. You'll never make a good typist if you can't do it by touch. Rhythm, it's all rhythm. Play it to music in your head."

So Lucy obediently looked away, and typed to a slow tune in her head, dum diddle dum dee, dum diddle dum dee . . . Why did her fingers feel funny? Why were goosepimples shivering her flesh? Was the typewriter really humming *in tune*?

She sat back, clasping her hands together, and stared at the letter in the machine. It read:

Dear Sirs,
 YOU ARE SITTING IN MY CHAIR to inform you that GO AWAY a new line of WE DO NOT WANT YOU HERE cushions in yellow, SILLY CHIT and pink. QWERTYUIOP.

She could not believe her eyes. She stared at the extraordinary words and trembled.

"Let's hope you stay longer than the other ones," the old man had said.

Tears came into Lucy's eyes. She tore the sheets out of the typewriter and threw them into the wastepaper basket. Then she put in fresh paper and began again. Grimly, in defiance of Mrs Price's teaching, she kept her eyes on the keyboard.

Dear Sirs,
 We are pleased to inform you that Ross and Bannister's have introduced a new line of Sunburst cushions . . .

With a rattle the typewriter took over. She felt the keys hitting her fingers from below, leaping up and down like mad children at playtime. She took her hands away and watched.

. . . YOU CAN'T KEEP ME OUT THAT WAY, the typewriter printed. YOU'LL NEVER BE RID OF ME. NEVER. WHY DON'T YOU GO. NO-ONE WANTS YOU HERE. NO-ONE LIKES YOU. GO AWAY BEFORE

Then it stopped, its threat uncompleted.

Lucy leapt up, overturning her chair and ran to the door.

"Left the same day she came," the old man had said. "Shot off like a scalded cat!"

"No!" Lucy shouted.

She left the door and went over to the window, looking down at the bright shops. She thought of jumble sales and baked beans. She thought of pretty new clothes and rump steaks. She might be young and shy and a little slow, but she was not, no, she was *not* a coward!

She went back and sat down in front of the typewriter and glared at it. There it crouched, like a squat, ugly monster, staring at her with its alphabetical eyes.

Lucy typed quickly:

Are you from outer space?

The typewriter rocked, as if with laughter, its keys clicking like badly fitting false teeth.

IDIOT, it wrote.

Who are you? Lucy typed.

MISS BROOME, it answered.

Lucy hesitated. She did not know quite how to reply to this. In the end she typed:

**117**

How do you do? I am Miss Beck.

GO AWAY, MISS BECK

Why should I?

I AM SECRETARY HERE, it stated, this time in red letters.

No, you're not! *I* am! Lucy typed angrily.

The machine went mad.

QWERTYUIOP!'/@QWERTYUIOP£-&()* QWERTYUIOP+! it screamed, shaking and snapping its keys like castanets.

Lucy switched it off. She sat for a long time, staring in front of her, her face stubborn. Then she took the cap off the bottle of correcting fluid.

For an hour, she battled with the machine. As fast as QWERTYUIOPs and unwanted capitals appeared, she attacked with a loaded brush. The white fluid ran down the typing paper like melting ice-cream, and dripped thickly into the depths of the typewriter.

YOU'RE DROWNING ME, it complained pathetically, and she swiped at the words with her brush.

HELP!

Another swipe.

PLEASE!

But Lucy showed no mercy. The large bottle was half-empty when she reached the end of the letter in triumph.

Yours faithfully,

George Ross, she typed, and sat back with a sigh of relief.

The machine began to rattle. Too late, Lucy

snatched the completed letter out of the type-writer. Across the bottom of the otherwise fault-less page, it now said in large, red capitals:

I HATE YOU!

Furiously she painted the words out.

Mr Ross came to the office at four o'clock. His eyes went to the corner of the desk where Lucy had put the completed letters. If he was sur-prised to find so modest a number after a day's work, he did not say so, but picked them up.

"Any telephone messages?" he asked.

"On your desk, sir," Lucy said and went to make him tea.

When she brought it in on a flowered metal tray, she found Mr Ross signing the last letter, his pen skidding awkwardly over the thick shiny layer of plastic paper. All the letters were heavily damasked with the dried fluid, like starched table napkins. He glanced up at her a little unhappily.

"Did you have trouble with the machine, Miss Beck?" he asked.

"Yes, sir." (She was afraid to say what trouble in case he thought she was mad).

"It's only just come back from being serviced," he said wearily.

"I'm sorry, sir. It keeps . . . going wrong."

There was a long silence. Then he said with a sigh, "I see. Well, do what you can. If it's no better at the end of the week . . ."

He let the sentence hang in the air, so that she

was not certain whether it would be the type-writer or Lucy Beck who would get the chop.

The next morning, Harry Darke raised his eyebrows when he saw Lucy.

"Still here?" he exclaimed. "Well done, my dear. I never thought I'd be seeing you again. You're braver than you look. Fighting back, eh?"

"Yes," said Lucy briefly. She walked past him and went up to the desk. *Her* desk. Then she took out of her carrier bag a small bunch of daffodils and a blue vase.

"Staking your claim, I see," the old man said, regarding her with admiration. "D'you want me to fill that for you?"

"Thanks."

He came back, carrying a tray.

"Though I might as well make us tea while I was about it," he said. "Here's your vase."

"Thanks."

"I'll be here till one o'clock today," he said, as she arranged her flowers. "Anything you want to know? Any snags come up I can help you with? Light bulbs changed. Fuses mended. New bottles of correcting fluid handed out . . ."

"Mr Darke," Lucy said, looking straight into his small, bright eyes, "who is Miss Broome?"

"Wrong question, Miss Beck."

Lucy thought for a moment, then said, "Who *was* Miss Broome?"

He beamed at her approvingly: "You catch on quick, I'll say that for you. In fact, you're not the timid mouse you look, Miss Beck. You're a right

120

little lion. Need to be, if you're going to take on Miss Broome. Tough old devil she was."

"Tell me about her," Lucy said, as they sat over their tea.

"She was old Mr Bannister's secretary. Been here forty-three years, girl, woman and old misery. Sitting there where you're sitting now, her back straight as a ruler, and a chop-your-head-off ruler, too! Her stiff old fingers tapping out the letters one by one, with her nose nearly on the keyboard, so short-sighted she'd become by then. None of your touch-typing for her! Every letter she stared in the face like it was a criminal and she the judge. You can't wonder she hates you young girls, with your fingers flying over the keys like white butterflies, and your eyes gazing out into the sunshine. They gave her the push, you know."

"After forty-three years?" Lucy said, shocked into sympathy.

"Well, she was past it, wasn't she? Of course, they wrapped it up in tissue paper. Gave her a brass clock and shook her hand and waved her goodbye. She didn't want to go. Didn't have anything worth going to – a bedsit, a gas ring . . . The old bag didn't have any family who'd own her. This place was her home, this job was all she lived for."

Lucy was silent. Her mother had turned Uncle Bert out once, after a row, shouting that she'd had enough of him. Six weeks later, she had asked him to come back. "He looked so lonely, so lost," she had told Lucy. "All by himself in that horrid little room, with the worn lino and the curtains all shrunk."

"Sorry for her, are you?" Harry Darke asked, watching her face.

Lucy hardened her heart.

"It's *my* job now," she said. "I need it. She can't have it for ever, it's not fair. It's my turn now."

"So it's a fight to the finish, is it, Miss Beck?" he asked, smiling.

"Yes," she said, and unscrewed the cap from the bottle of correcting fluid.

Her mother was working late that night. Lucy, going into the kitchen to get her own supper, was surprised to find the table neatly laid out with ham and salad, apple pie and a jug of tinned milk. Uncle Bert was sitting waiting for her, beaming proudly.

"Thought I'd have your supper ready," he explained, "now you're a working girl."

"Thanks," she said, but couldn't resist adding nastily, "I don't get paid till Friday, you know. No good trying to touch me for a fiver."

He flushed. "You don't think much of me, do you? Who are you to set yourself up as judge and jury? You don't know what it's like . . . not being wanted. A little kindness would help!"

Lucy noticed his hands were shaking. His collapsing face seemed held together in a scarlet net of broken veins. His eyes were miserable.

"Uncle Bert," she began.

"What?" He looked at her warily.

"I'm sorry. I'm sorry, Uncle Bert."

"I'm sorry, too, Lucy," he said. "I know it's a nuisance, having me here."

"No! No, it isn't! We want you," she said.

They smiled at each other timidly over the kitchen table, each remembering the little girl and the handsome uncle, who had once flown kites together in Waterlow Park.

Wednesday was Harry Darke's day off. Alone in the office, Lucy put a sheet of paper in the typewriter, and typed quickly:

QWERTYUIOP QWERTYUIOP QWERTY-UIOP.

The typewriter gave a jerk, as if surprised, and hummed.

Lucy typed:

Dear Miss Broome,

Mr Darke told me you used to be secretary to Mr Bannister . . .

I AM, interrupted the typewriter.

Lucy went on,

I am sorry to have to tell you that Mr Bannister [she hesitated, wondering how to put it,] . . . passed on three years ago, at the age of eighty-six . . .

LIAR! I DON'T BELIEVE YOU!

It is true, Miss Broome. I have seen his grave in the cemetery. It is not far from yours. I went along last night and left you flowers . . .

!!!!!

I did. Mr Darke is worried about Mr Bannister. He does not know how he will manage without you . . .

HE CAN MANAGE WITHOUT ME ALL RIGHT! said the typewriter bitterly, HE TOLD ME TO GO. BRASS CLOCK, WHAT DID I WANT WITH BRASS CLOCKS! I WANTED MY JOB.

They only asked you to go because they were worried about your health. [Lucy typed quickly.] Mr Darke told me Mr Bannister was always saying how much he missed you . . .

? ? ?

Truly. He said Mr Bannister complained none of the new girls were any good. There was no-one like you, he said . . .

The typewriter was silent. Sunlight glittered on its keys, so that they looked wet.

. . . He must miss you. He's probably in an awful muddle up there, mislaying his wings. Losing his harp. He needs someone to look after him . . .

The machine was silent. Lucy waited, but it said nothing more.

So she typed:

Goodbye, Miss Broome. Best of luck in your new job,

Yours sincerely,

Lucy Beck, Secretary

She folded the finished letter into a paper dart and sent it sailing out of the window. The wind caught it and carried it away.

Mr Ross is delighted now with his new secretary. Harry Darke says she's champion and gives her chocolate biscuits with her tea.

"However did you do it?" he asked.

## 10   The Masquerade

Everyone in Venice seemed to be in love. Everyone, that is, except Arthur Watson and his aunt Millicent.

They sat at a table in the sun, eating ice-cream; and watched the world walk by. Hand-in-hand. Two-by-two. The sun glittered on the water of the Grand Canal. On the far bank, old palaces, as pink and peeling as Aunt Millicent's face, dozed above their reflections. Now and then, a noisy river-bus scuttled by, its wake lapping against the tethered gondolas, so that they knocked against each other, like agitated elongated black swans.

"Venice in spring," Aunt Millicent said. "What could be nicer?"

Anything, Arthur thought. Give me the fair on Hampstead Heath, the disco at Camden Lock – and you can keep Venice!

But he smiled and mumbled something polite. It was kind of his rich aunt to treat him to this holiday abroad. He knew he ought to be grateful. It wasn't her fault that everyone staying at their expensive hotel was fat and old. It was just his bad luck.

He had so looked forward to this holiday. At fifteen, he was ready to fall in love. Given half a chance, a smile from a pretty girl and his heart would have been lost. He longed for a romantic adventure to boast about back at school. But no-one even looked at him. It was Aunt Millicent who collected the smiles.

If only she wasn't so fat. If only she wouldn't wear a pink dress covered with large black spots. She looked like an ice-cream sundae, with her bleached hair piled above a strawberry face and topped with a gondolier's straw hat, like a wafer done up in red ribbon. White letters on this ribbon announced: I LOVE VENICE. He could not help wishing she were invisible.

A pair of pretty girls were strolling by, the first he had seen unattached to young men. The dark one looked at his aunt. Her lips twitched. She turned and whispered something in her companion's ear and they both laughed.

I'd like to kill them, he thought, I'd like to shoot them dead.

Aunt Millicent too had been watching the girls. She did not seem offended by their amusement, but smiled at them kindly.

"It's a pity there aren't any young people at the hotel," she said. "It must be dull for you, going around with an old woman like me."

"No," he said politely. "I'm enjoying myself."

His face felt stiff with the effort of looking as if he were having a good time.

"Perhaps you'll meet someone on Friday," she said.

Friday, Arthur thought, and a spark of excitement lit in his gloomy mind. On Friday the hotel was having its annual ball. A Masquerade.

"The waiter said *everyone* has to wear masks," Aunt Millicent said. "Won't that be fun?"

Pictures filled Arthur's mind. Cloaked figures strolling through the narrow, shadowed lanes, voices laughing . . . He saw himself standing with a girl on the little bridge outside the hotel, listening to the sound of gondoliers singing in the distance. Watching the moonlight reflecting in the dark water. Then the sound of midnight bells, . . . a gloved hand lifting a mask to reveal . . .

"Wasn't it lucky I brought my pink chiffon?" Aunt Millicent asked happily.

. . . to reveal Aunt Millicent, Arthur thought bitterly. Who else would there be for him to dance with? Aunt Millicent or one of the other old bags.

"There's bound to be a lot of young people there," Aunt Millicent said, as if guessing his thoughts. "It's not just for the hotel guests. People come from all over Venice. We'd better go and choose our masks tomorrow, before all the best ones have gone. I noticed a shop selling them this morning. Proper carnival masks. Now where was it?"

\* \* \*

It took them an hour to find the shop again. The narrow crowded lanes all looked alike. All had shops selling Venetian glass; pink doves, golden horses, crimson goblets and speckled paper-weights. They might have been going round in circles.

"My feet are killing me," Aunt Millicent said dolefully. "If we don't find it soon, I'll have to give up."

But suddenly there it was, round the next corner. A narrow shop, filled with hollow faces; devils and monsters, nymphs and death's heads, gaping mouths, staring, empty eyes.

"Isn't this fun?" Aunt Millicent said.

She put a mask over her face and turned to Arthur, transformed.

It was a doll's face, with round glossy pink cheeks and a cupid's bow mouth. With her stout body beneath it, she looked like one of those painted Russian dolls that unscrew in the middle to reveal another doll inside, and another and another. Six Aunt Millicents, thought Arthur. Good grief!

"What do you think?" she said.

"It's super."

"Do you really think so?"

"Yes," he lied.

She turned back to the mirror and said wistfully, "Makes me look young again, doesn't it? Mutton masked as lamb. Well, why not, for once? I'll have it."

She handed it to the shopkeeper, who smiled,

said something in Italian, and began to wrap it up in tissue paper. Aunt Millicent's youth, Arthur thought, to be stored in moth balls till wanted again.

"Now you must choose one," she said.

He looked round the shop. What should he be? A devil? An angel? A monster?

"What about that lion's head?" Aunt Millicent suggested. "Or that dragon? Look, that gold one's rather handsome."

But somehow the grinning, painted faces did not appeal to him. They reminded him too much of his aunts at Christmas. He wanted something different . . .

"I'd like that one," he said suddenly, pointing.

"*That* one?" she said, looking at it doubtfully. "But it's so plain. Now you're not to worry about the price, Artie. It's on me. Wouldn't you rather have one of the coloured ones?"

The shopkeeper, an old woman with eyes like black olives, seeing Arthur pointing, had taken the mask down and now offered it to him.

"I don't know," Aunt Millicent said uneasily. "It looks a bit like a death mask.'

Arthur put it on. He looked at himself in the glass. The polite, round-faced schoolboy was gone. Beneath his own dark hair there was now a mysterious blank, paper-white. The eyeholes, black as ink blots, seemed empty. He was filled with an odd excitement, a sense of freedom. He had always hated his own face. It was so ordinary. Dull. Common. "He takes after my side of the family," his father had once said, and Arthur, looking round at his stout, red-faced uncles and fat aunts, had shuddered inwardly. He did not want to be like them. He did not want to be like *anyone*.

Behind the mask, he screwed his face up into horrible scowls. The white face in the mirror looked politely back at him, giving nothing away.

"It's a bit ... creepy," Aunt Millicent said uneasily.

"I like it," Arthur said. He turned to her suddenly and gave a deep elaborate bow. "Kindest and most beautiful lady," he said, weirdly, "will you give it to me?"

The mask hid his blush. What on earth had made him say that? She would think he was making fun of her.

But Aunt Millicent only giggled. "Get on with you, Artie! Of course you can have it. If you're sure it's the one you want?"

"Yes."

The shopkeeper said something suddenly in rapid Italian. They smiled at her blankly, not understanding a word.

"We'll take this one," Aunt Millicent said.

Arthur removed the mask and handed it to the old woman. She stood holding it, staring at him with her black eyes. Then she said something in a doubtful-sounding voice.

He spread out his hands. "Sorry. No comprendo."

"We want both of them," Aunt Millicent said.

"The two. Les deux, no, that's French. What's two in Italian, Artie?"

"Er . . . uno, due . . . Il due, I think."

"Il due," repeated Aunt Millicent, "Comprendo?"

The shopkeeper was still staring at Arthur with her dark, unsmiling eyes.

"*Sta attento!*" she said. "*Sta attento alla ragazza morta!*"

"Do you speak English?" Aunt Millicent asked.

The shopkeeper shook her head. After a moment she turned away, shrugging, and wrapped up the white mask.

"You can put them both in the same bag," Aunt Millicent said kindly.

Arthur could not stop looking at the mask. Alone in his hotel room that night, he tried it on again in front of the mirror. Once more he felt that odd excitement. The white face seemed to be waiting for something; like the blank page of a new diary promising a clean start.

He felt restless. Still wearing his mask, he walked out on to the balcony. Below him, he could see the dark water of the narrow canal that ran beside the hotel. There were the damp, stained landing steps, where every morning gondolas brought the provisions, piled high with fruit and vegetables, bread rolls and clean laundry. ("Oh look, Artie!" Aunt Millicent had said. "How romantic! Fancy having our coco crispies delivered by gondola.")

There was one coming now. Arthur leaned over

132

the balustrade and watched it approach. A girl was sitting on the cushioned seats. She had long red hair, shining like polished copper in the lamplight. Behind her, the gondolier bent over his oar, his face shadowed by his straw hat.

This is more like it, Arthur thought. This is the Venice I hoped for. Not all those boring churches and palaces . . . I wish I had the courage to thumb a lift.

"*Buona sera, signorina!*" he called out, surprising himself.

She looked up. Her face was pale, nearly as white as his mask, warmed only by her fiery hair. She was beautiful. And she smiled at him.

"Do you speak English?" he asked hopefully.

"Yes."

"Are you coming to the Masquerade on Friday?"

But the gondola was now passing under the bridge into the shadowed water beyond. Leaning out as far as he dared, Arthur saw a pale hand waving.

"Please come!' he shouted, and thought he heard her answer. Unfortunately she was too far away for him to make out the words.

He leaned on the balustrade for a long time, staring after the boat. She wouldn't have smiled at me, he thought, if I hadn't been wearing my mask. And he wondered if he had fallen in love.

On Friday night, the hotel was full of laughter, excited voices and quick footsteps. Aunt Millicent, swathed in pink chiffon and wearing her doll's mask, came out of room number 16 and pattered down the passage on high heels until she came to room number 21. She stopped, and knocked.

The door opened. A figure stood there like a shadow. Black hair, black sweat shirt, black trousers, black shoes. Only its face was white. A blank, expressionless face, oddly disturbing.

"Goodness, is that really you?" Aunt Millicent said. "You do look . . . You gave me quite a turn. Artie? Artie, it is you, isn't it?"

"Yes."

"Well, of course, who else could it be?" Aunt Millicent said, laughing at herself. "I must say, you look very . . . striking."

"My hands,' he said, holding them up, "my hands are all wrong."

She looked at them, puzzled.

"They look all right to me. Nice and clean, in fact."

"They're so red. So *meaty*."

"Nothing wrong with a nice bit of flesh," Aunt Millicent said, laughing. "Still, if it worries you, I can lend you a pair of white cotton gloves . . ."

The gloves fitted. The offending red hands were hidden. There was nothing visible of Arthur Watson.

Downstairs, the band had begun to play. Already the room was crowded. Everywhere grotesque figures capered and swayed to the music. A red devil's face grinned above a white lace dress. A bird with a golden beak wore tight blue denims. A lion flounced by in taffeta.

"Isn't this fun?" Aunt Millicent said.

A stout, red-nosed clown turned at the sound of her voice.

"Now, haven't we met before?" he said. "I'm sure I recognise that pretty face."

Behind her ridiculous mask, Aunt Millicent giggled happily.

That's her taken care of, Arthur thought, and slipped silently away. He was looking for the gondola girl, the girl with the long red hair. Masked figures surrounded him, squealing with laughter, babbling in a dozen assorted languages. Blondes, brunettes, blue rinses . . . Where was she? Perhaps she was not coming.

"Excuse me, excuse me," he said, pushing his way round the room.

A hand caught his arm. A voice said hopefully, "Hey, you're Bobby, aren't you?"

The girl's hair was short and fair. She was wearing a baby-doll mask.

"No. Sorry," he said.

"Oh, heck! Wrong again. At least you speak English. You're not John, are you?"

"I am no-one," he said; and felt suddenly cold. The white mask, the white gloves lay on his skin like ice.

"How'm I going to find them in this lot?" the girl asked ruefully. "Meet us in the dance room, they said. Darn it, I don't know what they look like now."

Her voice was warm and friendly. He felt a sudden impulse to claim that he was Bobby or John or whoever she wanted him to be. But he found himself saying again, "I am no-one."

Then a group of masked figures pushed between them. "Scusi, signor. Scusi, signorina." When he looked again, she was gone.

He was shivering. He felt odd. Was he going to be ill? His head felt light and his hands tingled. He held on to the back of a small gilded chair, and watched the dancers go past, round and round . . . I mustn't faint, he thought, I mustn't be sick.

A huge pink figure with bleached hair piled on top of its head was dancing past with a short, stout man.

"Aunt Millicent!" he cried with relief, pushing his way towards it. "Aunt Millicent!"

But when the figure turned, he saw the green wrinkled face of a monstrous ape.

"Sorry," he mumbled.

He was hot now. His face was burning behind his white mask. His hands were on fire inside the white gloves. He pushed his way out of the room. He tried to take off his mask, but his hands in the white gloves were oddly clumsy. He could not find the edge of the mask. He was stifling. He must get some air . . .

It was dark and cool outside. The reflection of a lamp bobbed like a golden ball in the dark water of the canal. By the landing steps, there was the long shadow of a gondola. Its arched metal prow gleamed silver in the dark.

The gondolier stood silently, holding the boat against the steps with his long oar. His face, beneath the shadow of his straw hat, was invisible. On the cushions in front of him sat the girl with the long red hair.

"You've come!" Arthur said. His head cleared. The burning shivery feeling left him. Lovesick, he thought, I must have been lovesick.

The girl stood up and stepped out of the boat. He saw she was wearing a long green cloak, which parted when she moved to show a delicate white dress beneath, like a bud opening.

She's beautiful, he thought. Then he saw with a slight shock that she was wearing a mask exactly like his own. The eyeholes in the blank white face were black as night. The paper lips, though slightly parted, concealed her own in shadow. He could not tell if she was smiling.

"I'm jolly glad you could come," he said.

"*Mezzanotte*," the gondolier said. "*Mezzanotte*." It sounded like a warning.

The girl glanced back. "*Mezzanotte*," she said, and sighed.

"What was all that about?" Arthur asked, as the boat moved away into the dark.

"*Mezzanotte*. Midnight."

"Is that when you have to go back?"

"Yes."

"Like Cinderella?"

137

She shook her head and said, with a touch of bitterness, "No prince."

Well, thank you very much, he thought, a little offended.

"What's your name?" he asked.

"Nulla."

"That's pretty. I'm . . ." he began, but before he could say his name, she put a gloved finger on the lips of his mask.

"Nulla," she said again. "Nulla."

"What?"

"Nothing. No name. Nothing."

So she wanted to be incognito! Perhaps she was the daughter of an Italian prince, slipping out of her palace at night to seek adventure. Or a film star, afraid of being recognised. His heart beat with excitement.

"Come and dance," he said.

She laughed and clapped her hands. "Dance," she repeated, and started pirouetting away from him along the path by the canal.

"Hey, it's the other way!" He pointed to the hotel entrance. "In here!"

"Dance," she said. "Come and dance!" She held out her hand in its long white glove.

He hesitated; then went towards her. Their gloved hands met. Music from the hotel ballroom reached them faintly as they danced. Light from the windows gilded their blankly white faces.

On and on they danced, through the narrow shadowed lanes, over the little bridges, through the moonlit squares of Venice. People turned to watch then as they passed. Someone called out something in Italian. An English voice said, "Oh look! How romantic!"

It *is* romantic, Arthur told himself. Like a dream, like a film. He half expected everyone to burst out singing. I am in love, he thought.

But somehow his heart remained cold and empty. To be honest, he wasn't really enjoying himself at all. He felt vaguely embarrassed. He tried at first to talk to the girl but her English seemed no better than his Italian.

"Do you live in Venice?" he had asked.

"No."

"Where do you come from, then?"

"Yes."

"I mean, where do you live?"

"No."

It was hopeless. In the end, he had given up and they danced in silence. He kept glancing at her through the eyeholes of his mask. He wished he could see her face. He didn't know what she expected. Was she waiting for him to kiss her? Or would she slap his face and scream if he attempted to? If only she would give him a hint. It was the first time he had been out with a girl, for you couldn't really count the girls at school. He tried to remember what the other boys said. "Chat 'em up a bit. Tell them they're pretty, and so on." If only she spoke English.

"You are beautiful," he said. "Bella."

"Yes."

"I love you."

"No."

Arthur made horrible faces behind his mask, and they danced on. It was really very boring. He began to long for midnight, when her gondolier would come and take her away. Still, at least he'd have something to tell them at school. "I met this extraordinary Italian bird," he'd say. "Didn't know the meaning of the word 'no' . . ."

The girl was dancing more quickly now, pulling him along at a rapid pace that made him feel quite dizzy. It must be nearly midnight. Probably she was afraid of being late. Her parents must be strict . . .

Now there was the dark water of a canal beside them again. He supposed they were going back to the landing steps. He tried to recognise the buildings, to look for his hotel, but they were going too fast. Everything blurred in front of his eyes; shadows, lights, the gleam of water . . . They were rushing through the night like cold wind.

Suddenly he was frightened. He tried to free his hand from hers, but could not.

"Stop!" he cried. "Please stop!"

"Dance!" she said, pulling him along even faster. "Dance!"

Then the chimes began. Midnight.

Her frenzied strength seemed at once to leave her. She stopped dancing and stood beside him, quivering in the cool air from the canal.

"Midnight!" he said with relief. "Time to take off your mask."

"No!"

"Oh, come on. Give us a kiss."

"No!"

It wasn't fair! After all that boring dancing . . . She had turned away from him, and he caught hold of her cloak, trying to pull her back.

"*Fuggi! Fuggi!*" she said. "Run away quick, poor little boy!"

It was the last straw. Furiously, he reached out and snatched off her mask.

"Oh God!" he screamed.

Her hair had come with the mask, the long red hair like seaweed clinging to a stone. And there was no face. No eyes, no mouth, nothing! For a moment her clothes remained standing in front of him, like a headless body. Then slowly they began to crumple and fall. He flung the mask down in horror. It fell face upwards – and there she was again, lying at his feet; the white face, the long red hair fanned out on the stone paving, the empty clothes taking the shape of a dead body.

Footsteps sounded behind him. People shouted. Whimpering with terror, he fled.

He ran blindly through the dark lanes, not knowing where he was going, only wanting to get away. Suddenly there were lights all around him. People. Small orchestras playing outside cafés. He was in St Mark's Square. He shrank

141

back. It seemed to him that everyone was staring at him. Quickly he turned away.

He nearly screamed again. From the shadows, white faces stared at him, blank white faces with eyes like ink blots. Then he realised they were only his own reflections. He was looking into the window of a shop selling mirrors. He was still wearing his mask.

He must take it off. It would give him away. They must be looking for a young man wearing a white mask. He tore off the gloves. Now his fingers found the edge of the mask easily. He ripped it off.

That was better. There were no white faces looking out of the mirrors any more. There was ... *nothing!* He leaned closer. Stared into the mirrors. Where was he? Where was his face? He looked down – *where were his hands?* Nothing! Nothing! No hands! No face!

Screaming, he ran into the square like a black shadow. People, strolling hand-in-hand, did not seem to hear him. He clutched at their arms with his invisible hands, and they never noticed. Laughing and talking, they walked on.

"Help me! Help me!" he shouted.

Then he saw Aunt Millicent, walking hand in hand with a stout, balding man, a fellow guest from the hotel. She had taken off her mask, and she was smiling. In the soft light, her face looked young again.

"Aunt Millicent! Aunt Millicent!"

She turned round. Looked this way and that, puzzled.

"I thought I heard someone calling," she said.

"Aunt Millicent! It's me! Help me!"

"Artie?" she said. Her eyes looked past him. Through him. "No, it's nothing," she said. "Funny. I thought I heard Artie for a minute."

"I'm not nothing! I'm me. Arthur Brown. Your nephew," he said, trying to claim himself back out of the empty air. "Your brother Tom's son. Remember me! I've got a round face. Snub nose. Pink cheeks. Dark hair. My hands are red and my fingers look like sausages – *and I want them back!*" he ended with a sob.

A sudden cloud of dust blew between him and Aunt Millicent. The tiny particles spiralled up into a column, coming together until they formed a hazy human shape. Astonished, he saw, made out of the dancing dust, his own round familiar face, the face he had once been so dissatisfied with. It seemed to look at him shyly, a little doubtfully, as if to say, "Shall I leave the dance? Didn't you know it was a dance of death? I thought you disliked me. Are you sure you want me back?"

"Artie?" Aunt MilLicent was saying. "Is that you?"

"Yes. Yes. It's me," he said gladly, and stepped forward into the strange dust. He felt it sting as it settled on his invisible face. He held out his hands imploringly, and saw to his delight two misty pink blobs forming in the air; solidifying,

143

turning back into the hands he thought he had lost for ever.

"Why, Artie, *there* you are! My poor boy, whatever's the matter?" Aunt Millicent said, and took him in her arms.

"I hate Venice," he sobbed. "I want to go home."

ALSO IN

Heinemann
*New Windmills*

Founding Editors: Anne and Ian Serraillier

**Chinua Achebe**  Things Fall Apart
**Vivien Alcock**  The Cuckoo Sister; The Monster Garden;
The Trial of Anna Cotman; A Kind of Thief; Ghostly Companions
**Margaret Atwood**  The Handmaid's Tale
**Jane Austen**  Pride and Prejudice
**J G Ballard**  Empire of the Sun
**Nina Bawden**  The Witch's Daughter; A Handful of Thieves; Carrie's
War; The Robbers; Devil by the Sea; Kept in the Dark; The Finding;
Keeping Henry; Humbug; The Outside Child
**Valerie Bierman**  No More School
**Melvin Burgess**  An Angel for May
**Ray Bradbury**  The Golden Apples of the Sun; The Illustrated Man
**Betsy Byars**  The Midnight Fox; Goodbye, Chicken Little; The
Pinballs; The Not-Just-Anybody Family; The Eighteenth Emergency
**Victor Canning**  The Runaways; Flight of the Grey Goose
**Ann Coburn**  Welcome to the Real World
**Hannah Cole**  Bring in the Spring
**Jane Leslie Conly**  Racso and the Rats of NIMH
**Robert Cormier**  We All Fall Down; Tunes for Bears to Dance to
**Roald Dahl**  Danny, The Champion of the World; The Wonderful
Story of Henry Sugar; George's Marvellous Medicine; The BFG;
The Witches; Boy; Going Solo; Matilda
**Anita Desai**  The Village by the Sea
**Charles Dickens**  A Christmas Carol; Great Expectations;
Hard Times; Oliver Twist; A Charles Dickens Selection
**Peter Dickinson**  Merlin Dreams
**Berlie Doherty**  Granny was a Buffer Girl; Street Child
**Roddy Doyle**  Paddy Clarke Ha Ha Ha
**Gerald Durrell**  My Family and Other Animals
**Anne Fine**  The Granny Project
**Anne Frank**  The Diary of Anne Frank
**Leon Garfield**  Six Apprentices; Six Shakespeare Stories;
Six More Shakespeare Stories
**Jamila Gavin**  The Wheel of Surya
**Adele Geras**  Snapshots of Paradise

**Alan Gibbons** Chicken
**Graham Greene** The Third Man and The Fallen Idol; Brighton Rock
**Thomas Hardy** The Withered Arm and Other Wessex Tales
**L P Hartley** The Go-Between
**Ernest Hemmingway** The Old Man and the Sea; A Farewell to Arms
**Nigel Hinton** Getting Free; Buddy; Buddy's Song
**Anne Holm** I Am David
**Janni Howker** Badger on the Barge; Isaac Campion; Martin Farrell
**Jennifer Johnston** Shadows on Our Skin
**Toeckey Jones** Go Well, Stay Well
**Geraldine Kaye** Comfort Herself; A Breath of Fresh Air
**Clive King** Me and My Million
**Dick King-Smith** The Sheep-Pig
**Daniel Keyes** Flowers for Algernon
**Elizabeth Laird** Red Sky in the Morning; Kiss the Dust
**D H Lawrence** The Fox and The Virgin and the Gypsy;
Selected Tales
**Harper Lee** To Kill a Mockingbird
**Ursula Le Guin** A Wizard of Earthsea
**Julius Lester** Basketball Game
**C Day Lewis** The Otterbury Incident
**David Line** Run for Your Life
**Joan Lingard** Across the Barricades; Into Exile; The Clearance;
The File on Fraulein Berg
**Robin Lister** The Odyssey
**Penelope Lively** The Ghost of Thomas Kempe
**Jack London** The Call of the Wild; White Fang
**Bernard Mac Laverty** Cal; The Best of Bernard Mac Laverty
**Margaret Mahy** The Haunting
**Jan Mark** Do You Read Me? (Eight Short Stories)
**James Vance Marshall** Walkabout
**W Somerset Maughan** The Kite and Other Stories
**Ian McEwan** The Daydreamer; A Child in Time
**Pat Moon** The Spying Game
**Michael Morpurgo** Waiting for Anya; My Friend Walter;
The War of Jenkins' Ear
**Bill Naughton** The Goalkeeper's Revenge
**New Windmill** A Charles Dickens Selection
**New Windmill** Book of Classic Short Stories
**New Windmill** Book of Nineteenth Century Short Stories

*How many have you read?*